THE DARK SEASON

NICOLLE MOROCK

Acknowledgments

Thank you to my friends and family who encourage me to keep writing and to Rayna's fans. Without your positive response, there would not be a sequel to *The Tritium Hypothesis.* Special thank you to Gayle and Maria for proofreading this story and catching the random errors and consistent misspellings because my eyes only see what they want to. Your attention to detail saved me again!

Special thank you to Nathan Ray for designing Rayna's original book covers.

This book is dedicated to Carol Turner Wenberg whose battle with ALS inspired me to finally finish writing it. I'm grateful you had the chance to read what Rayna did next before you passed. I miss you.

Read Nicolle's other books:

The Tritium Hypothesis

In Rayna Smith's world "normal" is a scientist sharing her home with an opinionated cat and a grumpy ghost. Things get weird when she's called to investigate a horse's unusual death on a nearby farm, a strange hum heard on a mountain across the valley, and her own UFO sighting - all in the same day! Can she, her friends, and a handsome forest ranger separate coincidence from design to help her small town get a grasp on the sudden influx of strange events?

Please, don't call me psychic. Stories from my paranormal life

For those who study the paranormal and metaphysical aspects of our world, psi refers to parapsychological phenomenon including extra sensory perception (ESP), precognition, and psychokinesis. Nicolle Morock has spent most of her life experiencing the paranormal. Over the last decade, she has investigated it as a member and Vice-president of the National Society of Paranormal Investigation and Research. Her most memorable adventures include

- An angry spirit throwing a temper tantrum in a hotel room while she slept
- The amorous ghost of a sailor leaving a heart-felt message on a digital recorder
- Walking into a private home that felt like it was in the middle of an energetic earthquake
- Being present when Saint Michael removed a dark spirit attachment from a friend.

These stories and more give the reader a glimpse into the reality of paranormal investigations and research.

Visit nicollemorock.com to find her latest work.

Chapter 1

Sam wasn't used to working in the office. He much preferred the quiet, distraction free environment of his own home in Jupiter. But there he was, sitting at his sterile desk, trying not to listen to the annoyance in the voice of his coworker at the *Weekly Courier*. She was beyond annoyed. With every sentence, her voice rose in pitch and volume, so he couldn't help but hear her side of the phone conversation.

"Ma'am, what do you mean rocks keep raining on your roof? Is somebody throwing rocks at your house?" She paused for a breath. "No? Then do you mean hail from a storm?"

Sam thought about it. There wouldn't be hail in late December in eastern Tennessee without some serious warmth. Being best friends with a meteorologist taught him that much. It had been bone-chilling cold for days. But the person on the other end of the line couldn't mean sleet either. The sun had been out for just as long as the cold had been there.

The reporter's voice kept going – asking partial questions and sounding more and more like an angry alley cat's. "Ma'am, if you think someone's breaking into your house… well, why don't you call the police? But you just said… If it's not a person, who?"

"A raccoon," Sam thought to himself.

"A curse? Listen, I'm not sure what… what you think I can do to help you." Her voice was lowering in exasperation now. "I'm a reporter. I cover local government affairs. I don't know anything about stones and curses. You've got the wrong number." There was another pause and Sam expected to hear the phone slam down on the desk. "Yes, this is the paper, but… I don't know who you should talk to. Definitely not me!" Her voice lowered another octave when

1

she finished with "Give me your phone number, and I'll see if I can find someone to call you back."

A moment later, instead of a slam, Sam heard a tap, then a sigh, and then an expected announcement to no one in particular, "I need a cigarette!" The petite reporter whose name he couldn't remember stormed passed him and down the hall toward the front door. She had only been working there a few weeks, and this was the first day he'd been in the office since she started. She was a spitfire, though. Her red hair reminded him of a meme he'd seen on social media about the stereotype of redheaded women: God gave you a warning sign when he gave me red hair.

There was enough in her side of the conversation to pique Sam's interest. After all, when he wasn't being a tall, dark, and burly beat reporter, he was quietly investigating the paranormal with friends. He stood up casually, stretched his arms up over his head, feigned a yawn, and strolled down the same hallway. "I'm heading out to get some coffee," he said over his shoulder, knowing the few people in the office that day didn't really care.

He blinked his eyes as he walked out into the bright sunlight and brisk air. The redhead was standing about five feet to his right, puffing furiously. Sam gave her his best warm smile, dimples and all. She tried to ignore him, so he held out his hand in the universal hand-shake symbol and said, "I'm Sam. Today's my first day in the office since you started."

She softened a bit and shook his hand. "Bridgette," she told him.

"It's nice to meet you, Bridgette." He smiled again and watched as the hint of a grin flashed quickly through her eyes. "Not here long and already getting calls from the crazies, huh?"

"Yeah," she confirmed. "She was definitely crazy. I mean she said that someone was dropping rocks on her roof, and they were coming through the ceiling, but nobody could see any damage on the roof. Then there was something about

2

people breaking into her house, but the cops couldn't find any evidence. So, she called me? Why on earth would she call me? What am I? A shrink?" She took a long drag as Sam waited. "That's what she freakin' needs! A shrink! Nobody believes in curses anymore. This is the twenty-first century for God's sake!"

"Curses?" Sam asked and raised an eyebrow.

"Yeah, she said she was cursed. Or her house was cursed… something. I don't know. I was just trying to get off the darn phone. I've got better things to do."

"I see." Sam gave her a moment to finish her cigarette. "I couldn't help but hear you ask for her number. Did you actually write it down, or was that just to get her off the phone?"

"Yeah, I wrote it. It's in the trash can under my desk. Fish it out if you want, but I'm not going there."

"Thank you."

"What do you want it for anyway?" She studied him carefully for the first time.

"I'm a bored beat reporter. I might as well make her happy and call her back, right?"

"Sure. Have at it." She dropped her cigarette and stomped it out with the toe of her boot. "It's freakin' cold out here. I've got to go." With that, she turned and walked toward the parking lot, her long red hair bouncing with each step.

We made it through another dark season. Time to turn back toward the light.

Rayna's older sister was interrogating her again. "Why would you write that in a Christmas card?"

"Because it sounds way more poetic than saying 'Happy Winter Solstice!' yet again." She answered defensively. "Besides, I only sent that to the people I thought would get it. Obviously, I was wrong about you."

"It just seems morbid," Dawn said. "Why can't you just be normal?"

"After 30 plus years, it seems like you should know by now that's not possible," Rayna told her with a smile in her voice. "Just be happy you're still on the Christmas card list and not on the lump of coal list, okay?"

"Whatever." There was a pause while Dawn thought of something more interesting to discuss. "Did you ask Wolf to come with you to dinner on Sunday?"

"Nope." Rayna looked around her small kitchen for an excuse to get off the phone. Her little black cat, Cloud, slept on the floor in a sunny spot. The stove was clean, and the fridge was full. Nothing. It yielded no good excuse to cut the new conversation short.

"Why not?"

"Because he's still visiting his family in Mississippi."

Ranger Steven Wolf was Dawn's new favorite subject. He and Rayna had been seeing a lot of each other since they met earlier that year, but nobody in the family had met him yet. She was dying to see who finally had her sister's long-term interest, and Rayna was doing her best to delay that meeting.

Dawn pressed on, "You *could* text him, you know."

"I'm not planning to. He and I agreed that his family time is their time, not mine. I'll ask him when he gets back."

"When will that be?"

"Late Saturday."

"Seriously? Do you expect him to say yes on short notice?" Dawn was incredulous.

"Not really, but he might surprise me."

Rayna's phone buzzed in her hand, and she looked at it with heartfelt gratitude. Sam was calling. "Um… Dawn, I have to go. I'll talk to you later."

"Okay," she said. "Tell Sam I said, 'hi.'"

Rayna tapped her cell phone screen to answer Sam's call. "Dawn says, 'hi.' What's up?"

Sam's voice had an unusual edge of enthusiasm to it. "How do you feel about curses?"

"Um," Rayna wasn't sure why he was asking. "I'm not a fan of GD, but some of the four-letter words are okay depending on the context. Why do you ask?"

"No, I mean good old-fashioned curses – like a hex put on someone in revenge."

Rayna took a quick moment to think about her answer. "As a scientist, it would not be logical for me to put stock in silly superstitions."

Sam laughed. It was a deep, friendly sound. "Well, it's a good thing you're not always logical."

Rayna smiled. "Really, Sam, why *do* you ask?"

Sam filled her in on Bridgette's side of the phone call just a few minutes before. "Intriguing, huh?" He asked.

"Did you call her, yet?"

"No. I wanted to see if you were interested in talking to her first."

Rayna didn't have to think too hard about that one. She rarely turned down a case, especially if it was more interesting than the everyday, run-of-the-mill strange noises in the middle of the night variety. "Call her."

"Yes, ma'am!" Sam said and immediately hung up. Rayna stared at the phone in her hand and thought about the last case her little team investigated. This one *had* to be simpler. There was no way it couldn't be.

Chapter 2

Vickerton, Tennessee, is a small village northeast of Bell Mountain. The drive from Rayna's home in Jupiter took about 35 minutes. There was no traffic that day. Other than a random tractor, there wasn't much traffic on any day out that way. Rayna guessed most of the residents were visiting family for the holidays because the road was more deserted than usual.

She hadn't been to Vickerton in a few years. The drive brought back memories of her sister punch-bugging her arm while they rode to church in the back seat of their father's old Ford Taurus. There weren't many Catholic churches in their neck of the woods, so they drove 45 minutes every Sunday to attend mass.

Thankfully, now there was a small church in Jupiter, although Rayna rarely attended. It wasn't that she didn't believe or had lost her faith. It was just hard to get motivated on Sunday mornings. It was her one day to sleep past 5:00 AM, which meant she often didn't awake until 9:00. Running her own private weather business meant being up and making forecasts long before her clients arrived in their offices. Sunday was truly her day of rest.

It was just one more thing that bothered her mother. The list was long – Rayna was in her thirties, still unmarried, not in a hurry to be a mother, and now, a fallen-away Catholic because she preferred sleep to mass. Rayna's argument was that falling asleep during mass was ruder than not going. Of course, it was a lame excuse in her mother's eyes, but sleep was important to someone whose workday always started before dawn.

The pothole Rayna's little red pickup truck bounced through jarred her back to the present moment. She was almost to the address Sam had given her. As she rounded a curve, she could see the little house on the corner. It was like she remembered – a small, four-room house on the corner of the main road and a farm's access road. The color was different now. She recalled a creamy off-white color, but today it was painted forest green. Rayna thought the brick-red front door was a nice contrast and gave it a warm, homey feel.

Rayna pulled into the driveway just to the left of the house. Sam's car wasn't there, yet, and she decided to wait for him to arrive before knocking. She hoped he wasn't far behind her. Sitting in the driveway could prove awkward if the homeowner was the impatient type. Rayna studied the house for a moment and then took a slow, deep breath. She held it for a second and then let it out slowly and focused on how her feet felt on the floor of the truck. After another deep breath, she felt grounded and closed her eyes.

With her lids lowered, she looked at the house again in her mind's eye. It was different than she remembered it and different from its current look. It was off-white with a dark-stained wooden door. There were no shrubs around it, but there was a huge, old oak tree looming over it from the backyard with dead branches full of cawing crows. She could hear their sounds so clearly that she opened her eyes to see if there were crows around. There weren't, but there was Sam's car pulling into the driveway behind her.

She looked at the house again. From her vantage point, there was no sign of an oak tree, nor any other large tree around the house. There were just a few shrubs on either side of the front door and a little, dormant sapling in the front yard. She looked in her rearview to see Sam getting out of his car, took another deep breath, and exited her truck to join him.

Sam always greeted Rayna with a hug. The two of them had been close friends since childhood. He was the big brother she never had, and she was nicer than his little sister ever had been, and smarter, too. "What do you think?" He asked.

"I'm trying not to think just yet," Rayna told him. "It's definitely an old place. I remember passing through here when I was a kid. It looked different back then."

As they walked toward the front door, it opened slowly. A short, dark woman peeked out. She had a multi-colored throw blanket wrapped around her shoulders over a gray sweat suit and house slippers. Strands of gray and black hair peeked out from under a blue knit cap. She smiled and motioned for them to come inside.

Rayna stepped into the home first and immediately held her hand out to the lady. "Hi, I'm Rayna. Are you Amanda?"

The woman shook her hand with a grip firmer than Rayna expected. "Yes, but call me Mandy, please." She looked up at Sam as he shut the door behind him. "Are you the reporter I talked to yesterday?"

He shook her hand as he answered, "Yes, ma'am. I'm Sam. It's nice to meet you."

Mandy led them further into the living room and motioned for them to sit in two well-worn chairs. Rayna quickly surveyed the room. It was cozy enough. There was an old couch that backed against the front window, a dark cherry coffee table, and the two floral fabric-covered chairs they were settling into. A fire crackled in the fireplace to their right. Behind them, she had noticed a door to what was probably the kitchen, and to their left was a door to what looked like a bedroom. She guessed the house was about 800 square feet and over a hundred years old. The scuffed hardwood floors slanted and there was a crack in the paint that ran along the top of one wall. Everything about the place felt ancient.

"It ain't much, but it's home," Mandy told them as she sat on the couch facing them. "It's paid for, and that's important to me."

Rayna smiled at her. "I like it!" she assured the lady. "Mine is only a little bigger, almost as old – I'm guessing – and not quite paid for."

"How old is this house?" Sam asked.

"It was built in the 1840s," Mandy told them. "At one point, my great-grandparents lived here. They worked the farm back there," she pointed toward the back of the house, "and they raised their children right here in this room."

There was a sense of pride in her voice. "They didn't own it, though," she added. "They rented it from the farmer. Eventually, he sold it out from under them, and they had to move into the village." She paused and studied Sam for a moment. Then she tapped on the arm of the couch for emphasis when she said, "I think they'd be happy that I came back here and bought their old home."

"Yes, ma'am. I'm sure they would be," he assured her.

"They loved it here," Mandy continued. "It was a quiet place to relax after a hard day in the fields. There was plenty of room for their kids to play in the yard, and there was an oak tree out back that gave them shade in the summer. My grandma used to tell me about that tree. The trunk was so big that she and her brother could hide from their parent's view just by standing on the other side of it."

Rayna continued to smile outwardly. She took a deep breath and re-grounded herself. Her vision was right. Somehow that always surprised her even though it happened more often than not. She imagined standing in front of the tree back then. It felt like a bright, happy place to be. Still, there was a darkness not far from it. Something somewhere just beyond it seemed to be casting a shadow that had nothing to do with the old oak's branches. She couldn't put her finger on where.

Mandy was still talking, her voice getting softer as she did. "After I retired from the bank, I decided to come back here and buy the place. It didn't cost much, which was nice. Of course, there ain't much to it." She nodded toward the fireplace. "If it weren't for that and the space heaters, I'd nearly freeze to death in the winter. Then I bake in the summer. Nobody ever put any HVAC system in here. Heck! I'm lucky someone added on a bathroom off the back at some point. You know? An outhouse isn't much fun in the winter."

Sam laughed lightly. "No, ma'am. It's not! How much would it cost to add an air conditioning system here?"

"More than I probably have right now," Mandy lamented. "The recession cost me most of my savings right after I bought this place. I had to start working again."

"You're still working?" Rayna asked, trying not to sound as surprised as she was. It was hard for her to tell how old Mandy was, but she guessed the woman was well into her 70s.

"I do bookkeeping for a few businesses in town," she answered. "It keeps the lights on and food on the table. I don't need much else."

Sam rubbed his hands together as if to warm them. "Ms. Franks, do you mind telling Rayna about why you called Bridgette at the paper?"

"Call me Mandy," she scolded. "Miss Rayna, are you the psychic friend Sam told me about?"

Rayna shot Sam a sharp glance. She hated being called psychic. It's such a loaded word. She quickly recomposed herself and answered, "I'm Sam's friend, and I'm... on the sensitive side, but please don't ask me to tell your fortune. That's not my thing."

"Oh," Mandy said and looked at Sam inquisitively. "I thought he was bringing a psychic."

"Rayna *is* the friend I told you about," Sam replied. "She's pretty good at figuring out what's going on when it comes to the paranormal. She's just not a fan of labels."

Mandy relaxed a little. "Oh, okay. I get that. I don't like labels either." She grinned briefly. "Some people have labeled me crazy."

"I assure you, Mandy," Rayna said, "I'm not a fan of using that label."

"Good."

Sam prompted her again, "Tell Rayna what's been going on here."

"Actually," Rayna interjected, "do you mind showing me around before you tell me? I usually do a quick, cold walkthrough so I can see what I pick up before I have the chance to be influenced by any stories."

"Oh," Sam said. "Right. We'll do a cold walkthrough if that's okay, Mandy?" He blew on his hands without thinking.

"Sure, sure." Their hostess said as she rose slowly from her chair. "Maybe I'll pick up a blanket for you, Sam, while we're up."

"No, ma'am. I'll be fine. Thanks," he said as they followed her to the room just to the right of the entryway.

Mandy stepped aside to let Rayna go in first. Rayna walked slowly around the room noticing details with her eyes and paying attention to any sensations she felt anywhere on her own body. It was obviously Mandy's bedroom, and it was tidy. The double bed was covered in a heavy quilt that looked handmade. There was a large, oak armoire on one wall and the door to a small closet on the other. A nightstand next to the bed had a lamp, reading glasses, and a Bible laying on it. Rayna didn't feel anything unusual in the room, so she nodded to Sam and they moved on to the next.

Behind the first bedroom was a mostly empty room that seemed to Rayna had also been a bedroom at one point. It was even colder, being the farthest room from the fireplace. There was an old roll-top desk next to the room's only window, but that was the only furniture she saw. Rayna felt a tingle on the back of her head as if someone was playing lightly with her brown hair. She brushed her hand over the spot but felt nothing. Sam and Mandy were still in the doorway between the two rooms, so it couldn't have been him messing with her.

He noticed her motion and asked, "You okay?"

"Yeah," she said, "I'm fine. I just got a little tingle."

Mandy asked, "A tingle?"

"I'll explain in a bit," Rayna answered. "Is this the bathroom?" She asked as she walked toward a doorway on the back wall.

"Yes."

Rayna stepped into the small room. She could tell it had been added long after the house was built because the wall it shared with the empty room still had the look of exterior siding. She closed her eyes for a moment and visualized what the world was like a hundred years before. The big tree was directly in front of her. There was a barn about 50 feet behind it, and some sort of clearing in the tall grass to the right of the barn and a little farther back. She took a deep breath, opened her eyes again and rejoined them in the empty room.

"The only room left is the kitchen," Mandy told them as she led them through a third doorway on an interior wall.

As they walked into the kitchen, Rayna could look to her left and see through another doorway back into the living room where they started. Mandy was explaining that she had replaced the oven twice since moving in. She wasn't sure why her appliances had so many issues. The electrical wiring had all been replaced by the last owners. Rayna half-heard her story, but she was distracted. Her attention was being pulled back to the living room and she wasn't sure why. She turned to look at Mandy and then it happened.

Out of the corner of her eye she saw a dark shadow, about the height of a child or maybe a short adult, dart past the doorway in the living room. She turned toward it, but it was gone. She quickly looked at Sam and drew a sharp breath.

"What?" Mandy asked.

"Yes, what?" Sam repeated.

"I'm not sure."

"You saw it, didn't you?" Mandy asked her.

"Saw what?" Rayna said.

"The thing."

Sam asked, "Thing?"

"I saw *something*," Rayna said. "It was about this high," she held her hand to the middle of her chest, "and it darted from the left to the right on the other side of that door." She pointed to the living room. "Then it was gone."

"I'm glad you saw it." Mandy said. "I was afraid you wouldn't see anything, and like everyone else, you wouldn't believe me."

Rayna walked back into the living room and looked around. The heavy curtains were closed, presumably to insulate the little house from the cold outside as much as possible. There was no way outside light could have made its way into that room through those curtains. She walked to the door of the front bedroom and noted the curtains in that room were shut as well.

With a shadow created by the reflection of a passing car ruled out, Rayna looked at the small TV in a corner of the room. It was off.

Sam and Mandy joined her in the living room. "What did it look like?" Sam asked her.

"It was a dark shadow and seemed solid somehow." She looked back at the doorway to the kitchen. It passed from left to right, so from this perspective, it would have been right to left." Her voice trailed off as she thought out loud and started walking back toward the kitchen. "Mandy, do you know if there was ever a door here?" Rayna pointed at the wall where it seemed to her the shadow would have emerged.

"I'm not sure," Mandy answered with some hesitation in her voice. She looked from Rayna to Sam and added, "This house is so old. It could have been different at some point."

"True," Rayna agreed.

Sam asked, "So, you've seen this shadow before? You called it `the thing'?"

"Yes," Mandy answered. "I usually see it move through right around that same spot. Sometimes I'm in the kitchen, and sometimes I'm in the living room."

"Are the curtains always closed when you see it?" asked Rayna.

The woman thought for a moment. "No, I've seen it in the summer with the windows open."

"So, this has been happening for a while?" Rayna asked.

"Oh, yes."

Sam wondered out loud, "Was this why you called the paper?"

Mandy walked back to one of the chairs and sat down. Rayna and Sam followed and sat on the couch. She seemed lost in thought for a moment before answering.

"The shadow is just part of it. I'm not sure how to explain it all. Well, I can't explain any of it." She smiled at them. "I'm not sure I have the right words to describe it all."

Rayna smiled back. "Use whatever words you think fit it best. I'll ask questions if I need clarity on anything."

"Okay," she said and took a deep breath. "I've seen that thing you just saw many times. Sometimes I feel like it's just hanging out in a corner watching me, even when I can't see it. Then there's the rocks on the roof." Her eyes darted from Rayna to Sam and back. "Rocks fall on my roof sometimes."

"Do you mean fall from your roof?" Sam asked.

"No, I mean *on* it. I'll be sitting in here minding my own business and start hearing banging on the roof. Not constant – just kind of random, but enough in a row to make me go look outside. They're just bouncing up there." She pointed up. "The first time it happened, I thought maybe some kids from one of these farms were playing a joke. So, I walked around the house as fast as I could, but nobody was out there. The next time, I ran from window to window inside because I could see the whole yard faster that way, you see?"

Rayna nodded in understanding and Mandy continued. "There was never nobody there."

"What did you do?" Rayna asked.

"I called the police. It took them darn near an hour to come out. They said it didn't sound like an emergency, and they looked around, but they didn't see anything. Just some pebbles up there. They said it was probably just kids playing a prank. I told them I looked and never saw any kids. They just made a note in their notebook and left."

Sam asked her, "Has anything else strange happened?"

"Sometimes I see red laser lights in here."

"Laser lights?" He repeated.

"Yes, like what you'd play with a cat with. You know – like a laser pointer."

Rayna questioned, "Do you see the whole beam when you see that? Can you tell what direction the light is coming from?"

"No," she answered quickly. "It's more like just seeing the spot it makes."

"Like on the wall or the floor?" Rayna asked.

"No, it's in midair. Like right here," she pointed her finger to the air in front of her face, "right in front of me. Not on a surface – just midair!"

"How long has all this been going on?" Sam asked.

"Since I moved in, I guess. Maybe before. Who knows?" Mandy's voice was starting to have a tinge of frustration in it.

Rayna leaned toward her and did her best to give a reassuring smile. "You're right. It could be something that predates your owning the house. Do you know the person who lived here before you?"

"No." The answer was quick and to the point. Then she just stopped talking and an uneasy silence settled over them.

Rayna felt a familiar tingle at the crown of her head and reflexively reached up to touch the spot. She looked at Sam to see if he had seen her movement, but he seemed to be focused on Mandy who was staring at her hands in her lap. Then they heard it.

Plunk. Tap, tap, tap, tap, tap. It sounded like someone dropped a little ball that bounced on the floor somewhere in the house.

Mandy's eyes grew wide when she looked up at Sam and Rayna. Sam looked toward the back bedroom, and before he could say anything, Rayna was heading in that direction. She reached the room and looked for anything on the mostly empty floor that might have made the noise. She saw... nothing.

Sam and Mandy joined her. Sam said, "It sounded like a marble hitting the floor and bouncing."

"Or something like that," Rayna said as she crossed to the threshold of the little bathroom and scanned that room's floor, too. "Where was it, though?"

Mandy slowly got down on her hands and knees to see the floor more closely. "There you are!" She reached under the desk and retrieved a small marble. It was dark red and somewhat transparent. "How did you know that sound, Sam?" She asked as she struggled to stand back up.

He reached down and helped her rise while he answered, "I used to play with them when I was a kid."

Rayna stared at him with a cocked eyebrow. "You played marbles?"

"Yeah, why?" He held his hand out, and Mandy dropped the marble into it so he could examine it.

"I just didn't know that. I thought I knew everything about you," Rayna answered.

"Not everything. Just enough." He gave her a devilish grin before turning his attention back to the little ball in his hand. "Mandy, where did this come from?"

"Last time I saw it, I had put it inside the desk drawer. That top middle one." She pointed to it first, then opened it for good measure. "Yep. That's the one. It's not in there anymore."

Sam examined the desk drawer. It had been closed the whole time and there didn't appear to be any holes in it. He pulled it out as far as he could to see if the back of it was solid. "How old is this thing?"

"The desk? It belonged to my parents. It might go back to my grandma, but my mind's a little fuzzy on that part. It's just old." She paused. "I have no idea about the marble."

"What do you mean?" Rayna asked.

"I mean it's not mine. I don't know where it came from, but I keep finding it in strange places. I put it back in that drawer and then it shows up somewhere else."

"Do you put it back in the same drawer every time?" Sam asked.

"Not every time. Just the last few times." She took the marble back from Sam and put it into the drawer.

Rayna came closer. "Do you mind if I take it for a day or two?"

Mandy took the marble back out of the desk and handed it to Rayna. "Be my guest."

"Thanks." Rayna looked around the room again. "When you find the marble, is it always in here?" She motioned to the mostly empty space.

"No, girl. I've found it in the kitchen, the bathroom, the bedroom, and the living room. One day I even found it out back."

"Where was it the first time you found it?" Sam asked.

"Oh, I was sitting in the living room and heard something in the kitchen. At first, I thought it was a pebble hitting the window, but when I looked around, I found it on the floor near the back door."

Rayna looked at the little ball in her hands. "And you'd never seen it before then? When was that?"

"It was last spring. No, I'd never seen it. I thought maybe one of the grandchildren had left it here, but my daughter says they've never had any marbles."

"Interesting," Rayna put the marble in her jeans pocket and felt a twinge of anxiety. "I promise to return it," she said.

"You can keep it," Mandy told her.

"No, I don't think I can." Rayna replied and then changed the subject. "I know it's cold outside, but do you mind showing us around your property? Then we'll be on our way."

"Sure. Let me find some warm shoes." She shuffled to her bedroom.

Sam took the opportunity to whisper to Rayna, "What do you think?"

"There's definitely something going on here."

Mandy's voice called from the other room, "We'll go out the front door." They obeyed.

Chapter 3

The front yard was pretty neutral energetically in Rayna's mind. She had passed it so many times in her childhood that it was just part of the landscape. She remembered wondering who lived there and thinking about how small the house was, but she couldn't recall any strong feelings of trepidation or anxiety about it.

Mandy led them around the side of the house to the back yard. Although it had been gone for decades, Rayna could see the dip in the earth where the old oak tree once stood. About 50 feet beyond, there was an old barn that had seen better days. It wasn't falling apart, but it needed some tender loving care. As they approached, Rayna could tell by the peeling paint that it had once been dark green – many layers ago. There was a sensation of someone inside it watching them approach that made Rayna pause mid-step.

Sam noticed. "What?" He asked her quietly, but still loud enough to make Mandy turn to look at them.

Rayna took a breath and grounded again by focusing the feeling of her feet on the earth. She shook her head. "Nothing." It wasn't true. She still felt it, but she didn't want to worry their host. It took a bit of nerve to keep moving forward because the feeling was that they were intruding and unwelcome. Rayna hated when she got that feeling. It was the feeling that made her younger self afraid of shadowy places, and although she was now an adult and a paranormal investigator, she was still an empath. Those strong feelings still made her anxious, but now they also increased her curiosity.

With Mandy and Sam's attention back on the barn ahead of them, Rayna whispered almost silently, "Who are you?" There was no answer, but the sense of anger weakened slightly.

Soon they were standing in the doorway of the old building. It was mostly empty, except for a rusty old tractor and a few bales of hay. Rayna could tell it once held horses and possibly other livestock. Now it was just storage.

"Do you own the barn?" Sam asked.

"I do," Mandy said. "Although, I don't have much use for it. The farmers – my neighbors behind me pay me a little every year to use it for storage. Sometimes, it's full of hay. Sometimes, it's extra equipment. This time of year, they don't need it much."

Rayna stepped inside a few feet and looked around. With the only light coming from the sun behind her, most of the edges were cast in shadows. One corner seemed darker than the others, and the scientist in her told her it was her imagination. The nervous child inside her gave the corner a small quick wave hello. If there was a presence there, she was going to be friendly toward it.

She turned to ask Mandy a question, and there was a loud pop from that same corner that made all three of them jump.

"Barn cat?" Sam asked.

"Not that I've ever seen," Mandy answered.

Rayna turned back to face the corner and squinted into the darkness. "No, definitely not a cat." She kept her eyes focused on the darkness, hoping they'd adjust enough to let her see some detail. "Mandy, have you had any experiences in here?"

Mandy's answer was almost a whisper. "Sometimes, I get a little creeped out when I'm near the barn, but I try not to come in here for anything." She paused. "It's like they don't want me here."

"I see," Rayna said. Her eyes still couldn't make out any shapes in that dark space, so she turned back to Mandy again. Before she could remember the

22

question that had been on her mind before the popping sound, she noticed an emblem carved into the wooden door behind the woman. "What's that?" She pointed and walked over for a closer look.

The symbol looked like it had been both carved and somehow burned into the old wooden door. The outside of it was a nearly perfect circle, and inside, it looked like a rudimentary flower had been drawn. It seemed incredibly familiar, yet Rayna couldn't place it.

"That's part of why I don't come in here," Mandy said. "I think that has to do with witchcraft."

"Huh?" Sam stepped closer and traced the shape with his finger. "Maybe. I mean as old as the barn is… who knows? Is this why you mentioned a curse to Bridgette when you called the paper?"

"Yes," she answered without further explanation.

Rayna took her phone out of her pocket and took a couple of photos. "I'll see if I can find it in one of my books. I'm pretty sure I've seen it before somewhere."

"Okay," Mandy said. "Can we move on? I don't want to stir anything up."

"Sure," Rayna nodded. She and Sam closed the barn doors as Mandy started walking around the right side of the building.

She led them back another 25 feet behind the barn and a little off to the right. Rayna could see a short, iron fence that was all too familiar to her and anyone else who grew up in rural America. It was a family cemetery.

The stones were all weathered, and the names and dates had worn away, so it was hard to read any of them. "Is this your family?" Rayna asked.

"I think a few might be, but most of my ancestors wouldn't have had the pleasure of being buried in a proper graveyard. It's more likely they were interred in the woods behind the farm with just a large rock placed near their head for a marker."

Sam nodded. "Most slaves didn't have funerals or plots, so to speak."

"Right," Rayna said softly. "I knew that."

"My great-grandparents are buried in the black folk cemetery in the village." Mandy pointed toward town. "They didn't get to stay here, so they wouldn't have been buried here."

"Where are your grandparents buried?" Sam asked.

"Oh, they ended up in Jupiter in that little nursing home near downtown, so they got buried in that town's cemetery. My parents are there, too. Have you seen it? It's a nice one."

Rayna nodded again. "Yes," she answered. "My dad is there, too."

"Oh," Mandy said. "I'm sorry."

Rayna forced a smile. "That's okay. I was pretty young when he passed." She motioned to the gravestones in the space in front of them. "Is there any record of whose these are?"

Mandy answered, "I'm sure there is, but I don't have it. This part of the property belongs to the neighbors. I just thought you should know it's back here."

Rayna looked up at Sam and asked, "Got any tracing paper on you?"

Sam patted his jacket and jeans as if to check. "Nope. I'm fresh out."

"We'll bring some back," she told Mandy." I am curious as to who's here. It might help clue us in to what's going on."

"Oh, so you do think something's going on?" Mandy asked with a little excitement in her voice.

"Yes, ma'am," Rayna answered. "I'm just not sure what. I'd like to return with some tracing paper and equipment if you are interested in having us investigate."

"Oh, of course! When are you coming back?"

Sam looked at his watch absently. "How about Saturday?"

Mandy nodded. "That should be fine. Can I have my daughter join us? She'll be interested in meeting you."

Rayna answered, "We'd be happy to meet her, too."

They said their goodbyes as they walked back to the driveway. Rayna took one last look at the barn before getting into her truck. There was something in there that thrived on bad feelings. She was sure of it. The question was what. Or who?

Although Sam and Rayna had driven separately, they discussed Mandy on the way home using their cell phones. Rayna's sat on the passenger seat on speaker phone while Sam used a Bluetooth device. He teased her for her lack of technology in the old pickup, but she preferred simpler vehicles because there were fewer expensive parts to replace when things broke.

"What do you think was going on there?" Sam's voice carried over the sound of the pickup's heater on full blast. "Poltergeist?"

"That depends on which definition you're going with today," Rayna practically yelled so her friend would hear her clearly. "I don't think this is psychokinesis. I've felt that before, and this wasn't the same vibe." She heard a chuckle through the phone.

"Okay. You're going to have to explain that to me. What does PK feel like, for real?"

"Don't you remember when I told you about the lady's house down near the old fort?"

"Refresh my memory."

Rayna sighed quietly and wondered if Sam would ever remember the cases he didn't investigate with her. She'd update him throughout the investigation, but if he wasn't there, it's like it never happened in his mind. "The minute I walked through the front door, the whole place was vibrating so badly that it felt like an energetic earthquake. It was crazy, and it took a while for me to get used to it."

"Oh, yeah. The earthquake house." Maybe he did remember this one. "But how did you know it was PK?" Or maybe not.

"I didn't at the time. I just knew it wasn't evil, but a few months later, I was at a talk given by a guy who practices psychokinesis and when he demonstrated his abilities, it felt the exact same way. Now I know how to identify it."

"So, today was not an earthquake?"

"Nope."

There was a pause as they came to the stop sign on the east side of Bell Mountain. She watched as Sam's head moved to the left and right a few times before making the left turn toward Jupiter. Then he spoke again? "So, is it the other kind of poltergeist – the traditional noisy ghost?"

"I'm not sure. That's why I told her we'd bring the team out." Rayna made the turn cautiously. Sometimes teenagers used the road around the mountain to pretend they were racecar drivers. The blind curves had proven deadly often enough to warrant a long pause at that stop sign every time. "I figure we'll ask Barb and Fieldman if they're interested."

"What about your ranger?"

Rayna gave a quick laugh. "Why can't you just call him Wolf? Or Steven? Why does it always have to be 'your ranger' with you?"

"Why do you think?"

Rayna hoped Sam could see her roll her eyes in his rearview mirror. "Because it bothers me?"

"Maybe. So, are you going to ask him?"

"That depends on whether he'll be back in town when we decide to do it. I'd rather plan around the team and ask him later." She wasn't sure he'd be interested. The area had been pretty quiet with respect to paranormal stories since the event that brought them together. She had appreciated the calm period after all the craziness of those few weeks. It gave Wolf a chance to see her as more than the weird weather girl that lived with a ghost and saw UFOs.

Of course, the fact that they had experienced a close encounter together gave her a bit more credibility than she would have had otherwise. He had many questions on those first few dates after that, and she answered the ones she could. When she didn't have a solid answer, he was satisfied with "I don't know, but that's why we study these things – to see if we can find out."

Sam was talking again. "Rayna? Did you hear me?"

"Um, no. I think you broke up." She didn't want to admit her mind was on her ranger.

"Do you want to go back to Mandy's Saturday? Does this need to be an all-nighter, or are we good with the daytime thing?"

Rayna yawned just thinking about doing an overnight investigation. Early morning work plus late nights sitting in the dark asking questions of the empty air made for a very tired meteorologist. "I'm willing to put it up for a vote by whomever wants to join us." She hoped they'd vote for daylight.

Even with full sun, the darkness in the barn would be there.

Chapter 4

Rayna spent the rest of the day updating her accounting software and checking her phone obsessively for a text from Wolf. They'd only been dating a few months, but she'd grown accustomed to him being part of her life. She missed him when he wasn't around. She missed his smile, his wit, his smell – an outdoorsy, but clean scent, and mostly she missed his hugs. When he put his arms around her, the whole world disappeared and nothing else mattered. She hoped he missed her, too, but she wondered if that was likely since he hadn't texted all day.

Then she reminded herself that she was the one to set the ground rules for his time away visiting his family. She was the one who told him that he should relish his time with his mother and not waste it texting or calling her. She wished she had kept her mouth shut. How could she have known she was dating the one guy on Earth who would actually take her advice?

She checked her phone again, uselessly, and then stared through the blinds into the front yard. The sun was already setting, and the room was getting dark. It was going to be another frigid night in the valley. The heat had been running all day, and Rayna dreaded next month's energy bill. The upgrades she'd made to the house helped seal out some of the cold, but a nearly one-hundred-year-old house can only be so airtight.

Plunk. Tap, tap, tap. A blur of black fur when flying through the room. Cloud was on it – batting the thing across the floor, through the doorway, and down the hall. Then, there was an instance of silence, a plaintiff meow, and as fast as she'd left, Cloud was back in the room, cowering at Rayna's feet. It all happened so fast that Rayna didn't even realize she'd stood up.

"What the…" She looked down into her scared cat's green eyes and thought for a second. She knew that sound – the plunk. The marble. But how did it end up on the floor? She had put it in the shallow bowl near the front door where she kept her keys. And now... it was down the hallway?

Rayna took a deep breath and steeled her nerves. Grumpy, the spirit of a former owner of the house had been quiet the last few weeks. This didn't *feel* like him, but she spoke to him for good measure, "Not funny, Grumpy. Stop scaring my cat."

The light beside the couch turned on by itself. There was no click — just light. *That* was Grumpy. Cloud looked toward the lamp and seemed to relax, which told Rayna the marble's actions were caused by something else. She breathed deeply in again and let it out slowly. She imagined herself surrounded in white light and with a little more power and a touch of irritation in her voice, she said, "Who's here? What do you want?"

She waited in silence for a solid 30 seconds, but there was no response. "Fine," she said in an annoyed tone and walked toward the hallway. She turned the hall light on and scanned the floor. Her hallway ran from the front door, straight through the house to the back door. There were two bedrooms and a bathroom between the front of the house and the back. One bedroom was hers and the other she called Grumpy's. She walked down the hall toward the back door. She could see through its window that twilight was giving way to darkness, but the hall light showed her more of her own reflection through the window than any detail outside. At that moment, even her own reflection was giving her a twinge of anxiety.

Rayna looked down toward the door frame and saw the red marble resting against it, motionless. She bent down to pick it up and examine it. It felt ice cold to her fingers, and she moved her other hand along the bottom of the backdoor. She expected some leakage of cold air, but there was nothing. The marble was colder than the floor or the door.

"No one is allowed in this house if they are not of the light. Do you hear me? If you are not of the light, leave now." Her voice was as forceful as she could make it. "I do not have patience for darkness. If you're not of the light, you *will* leave."

Again, she stood in silence, waiting for something – anything to happen, but nothing did. So, she walked back to the front room to check on Cloud. The cat was sitting on the couch next to the table where the lamp was still lit. She seemed a little on edge, but less frightened. Rayna decided to leave the lamp on. It was often Grumpy's way of telling her he was around, but never meant much more than that. This evening, though, it seemed a little comforting.

She sat down on the couch next to her sweet little cat and rested her hand on her back. She felt Cloud relax a little more and then start to purr. The threat was gone, but what was it?

Rayna jumped when the phone on her desk rang, but she wasted no time composing herself when she recognized Wolf's ringtone. "Hello?"

"Hello," he sounded very formal. "I'm calling to get a weather report, please. I'd like to know if it's warm where my sunshine is."

Rayna chuckled. "It's never warm enough without you." Sappy. Sweet. Possibly embarrassing if anyone else was listening, but Cloud didn't care. "How's it going?"

"It's going pretty well. Mom's happy to have me home for a while. I don't think she wants me to leave. She keeps telling me there are plenty of parks in northern Mississippi to work at." Rayna could hear a smile in Wolf's voice while he spoke. "I guess I've been away too long, and I'm feeling a little guilty."

"Are there plenty of parks there?" Rayna said, hoping the answer was a firm no.

"Yes, but that doesn't mean I want to work here." She let out a quiet sigh of relief, and he kept talking. "I'm still planning to come home, but she's trying to get me to ask my manager for a few more days."

"I can understand that. I miss you when you're gone, too. Plus, she's your mom. She's *supposed* to miss you!"

"I told her I'd call him, but not to expect too much. I've already had a nice long holiday break while the other guys have had to work extra hours to cover for me."

"Did you call him?"

"No, I called you."

Rayna smiled and took a second to appreciate that fact. "You should call him and make her happy."

"I will. I just wanted to hear your voice for a minute. Sorry. I tried living by your rules, but I had to break the big one. I didn't want to wait anymore."

"Well, it was more of a guideline, I guess," she said with a grin. "I'm not mad at all."

"So, what's going on up there?"

Suddenly, the memory of the stress of just a few minutes before Wolf called rushed back to her. She inhaled slowly, and he heard it. "Well…"

"Did I interrupt something?"

"No, I was just sitting on the couch with Cloud when you called."

"So, what's up?"

"Let's just say I'm suddenly wrapped up in a case, and I might have brought something home with me." There was a long pause, and Rayna was afraid she shouldn't have said anything.

"I see. Did you tell it to go back to where it came from?"

"Not exactly, but I told it that it couldn't stay here." She appreciated that Wolf was so open-minded about her experiences. "Things had just calmed down when you called. Good timing!"

"Ha-ha! I guess I knew you needed me."

"At the risk of sounding corny, I always need you." As soon as Rayna said it, she second-guessed herself and tried to backtrack. "I mean, I don't need…" What should she say? You? A man? Anything?

"It's alright," he stopped her. "You're allowed."

And there it was – the whole reason she did – and at the same time did not – want to introduce him to her family. He was perfect, and she didn't want to scare him away with a big step like that. "Thank you."

"You're okay now though, right?"

"Yeah," she looked at Cloud – her spirit barometer stretched out with her chin resting on the couch. "I'm good. It's gone."

"Cool. Alright then, I guess I should call my boss and see what he thinks about my mom's request to keep me a few more days than planned."

"Let me know how that goes."

"Of course!"

There was a long pause, and Rayna wasn't sure if that was the end of the conversation. "Okay," she finally said.

"Okay."

"I guess… um… have a good night."

His voice was warm when he said it for the first time. "I love you."

Her voice caught in her throat. "I... love you, too."

"Goodnight."

"Goodnight."

She didn't hang up. She let him do it as she stared at her phone, letting it sink in. Then she gave a little squeal, and Cloud's head popped up with a start, her green eyes curious. "He said he loves me!" The little cat set her chin on her front paws, satisfied that nothing was wrong. "Sorry, Cloud. Didn't mean to startle you. I mean... wow! Yay! I mean... what's not to love, right?" She laughed.

Chapter 5

When Rayna finished her work the following day, she headed down to the sheriff's office to meet her best friend for a late lunch. She, Barb, and Sam had basically grown up together in their small town. After graduation from high school, Sam and Rayna went off to college and Barb stayed close to home and earned a two-year degree at the local community college. She landed the job with the county not long after that and had been in administrative positions ever since. Sam became a small-town journalist and loved it, and Rayna became a slightly larger town television meteorologist, which she hated. Straight hair and heavy makeup made her feel like a clown. She spent a few years privately wishing could just be her full authentic self until Sam and Barb convinced her to try her hand at private weather forecasting instead. They weren't even sure what the phrase meant, but they believed in her and they hated how miserable she seemed even though she had what everyone else called a "dream job."

Their encouragement and her love of forecasting pushed her to take a leap of faith. She lined up her first two corporate clients and put in her notice at the TV station, and she never looked back. Now she could live in her hometown, work as much as she wanted, wear sweats to work in her home office, and skip the heavy eyeliner and lipstick. She wasn't making a ton of money, but she made enough to stay financially independent and sock a little away each month for retirement.

Barb was waiting just inside the main entrance of the building, bundled up as if she were going skiing, or maybe just going to be eye candy in a ski lodge – grey swishy pants, white puffy coat, blonde hair tucked under a pink knit cap, and gloves that made her hands look twice their size. She was adorable, and somehow, she made all that extra fluff look stylish.

By contrast, Rayna wore her dark, curly hair loose under her blue hooded coat, and her blue jeans and light blue, off-brand winter boots had seen better days.

As much as she hated the cold, she refused to spend any extra money on winter wear. They lived far enough south that it usually didn't stay frigid long enough to warrant the extra expense. This week was something else, though. The Arctic air burned her face and made her wish she lived in southern Florida.

The Stay-Puft Marshmallow Barb gave her a cushioned hug. "Hi, Rayna! Cold enough for ya?"

"Not funny," Rayna smiled. "You look like you're ready to hit the slopes!"

"Too bad I don't have a ski date," Barb said and glanced over her shoulder at one of the cuter deputies. He nodded at her and Rayna and looked away.

"Him, too?" Rayna whispered.

"Nah!" Barb didn't whisper. "He's too young for me." Then she laughed. "I never thought I'd say that."

Rayna smiled. "Okay, Cougar, where do you want to eat?"

"The good diner, of course! You can drive."

"Drive? It's barely two blocks away."

"I'm not walking in that cold!"

"Then why are you wearing..." Rayna pointed and gestured widely at Barb, "all that?"

"To get me to your car in comfort."

Rayna rolled her eyes and pulled her keys out of her purse. Who was she to argue with a non-skiing ski bunny?

The lunch crowd had already gone back to work, and Barb and Rayna had the diner to themselves. They settled into the farthest booth from the door and stripped off their outer layers. Rayna noted how the open kitchen concept did much to keep the place on the toasty side.

Barb pretended to read the menu while asking, "So… when is Wolf coming home?"

"Hm… not sure," Rayna answered. "His mom wants him to stay a little longer, but his manager has the last word. Or maybe his coworkers who have to cover his shifts get the last words." She shrugged.

Barb set the menu down. "You miss him, don't you?"

"You know it."

"Of course, if he stays longer, that gets you out of taking him to dinner at your mom's house, right?"

"For now. It's going to happen sooner or later."

"Big step, huh?"

"Huge." Rayna looked around for a waitress. "I'm going to change the subject now."

Barb smirked. "Only if I let you."

"How would you like to investigate a haunted house and barn this weekend?"

"Ooh, okay. I'll let you change the subject." She leaned in and whispered, "Where?"

"Not far. It's over in Vickerton."

"And who says it's haunted?" She was still whispering.

Rayna looked around again and answered in full voice, "I do."

Barb leaned back and cocked her head. "You're sure about this one already?"

"Sam and I did a pre-investigation interview yesterday with the owner. She's sweet and she's having a hard time with something, or more than one something, maybe." The waitress interrupted, took their order, and disappeared again. "Finally," Rayna said, "I was starting to get a little hangry."

Barb nodded, "Yeah, and you were saying? Maybe more than one ghostie?"

"I actually saw something in the house that the homeowner, Mandy, apparently sees pretty regularly. We had a good bit of activity while we were there, and we weren't there very long."

"Sweet!"

"Then, there was something different and darker in the barn."

"Darker? Like a shadow person, or something?"

"I don't know. It felt bigger and like it didn't want to be seen and it definitely didn't want us there."

"So... we're going there?"

"If you want to join us, yes."

Barb leaned back in her seat and thought about it. "Is this barn heated?"

"Nope!"

"Would we be investigating at night or during the day?"

"I honestly see no reason not to do it during the daytime. Both were obviously active in the middle of the day while we were there. And given the forecast for another colder-than-normal weekend, a nighttime investigation of a barn with no heat seems brutally stupid in my professional opinion."

"Agreed."

"So, you'll come?"

Barb nodded. "Who else will be there?"

"Probably just Sam. I don't think Fieldman is interested in this one. He's got a lot going on right now."

"What about Wolf?"

"If he's home, he's welcome to come, but I have a feeling he's staying in Mississippi a while longer."

She nodded again. "Well, I guess somebody has to keep you and Sam in line. I'm in!"

"I probably don't have to tell you to dress warmly, but I might remind you that swishy fabrics are a bad idea for audio recordings."

A quick frown crossed Barb's face. "Okay, fine. Cold weather, no heat, and quiet fabrics. I can do that. I have *lots* of fleece!"

"And all of it's pink." Rayna teased.

After lunch, Rayna and Barb returned to the Sheriff's office where Rayna asked one of the lounging deputies his opinion on some of the things Mandy said she'd told her own county's deputies. The officer was around 40 years old with thinning brown hair and a little gray in his beard. He listened intently to Mandy's reported experiences of pebbles hitting the roof and the windows with no one in sight and no footprints or other evidence of people nearby.

"I know, Miss Rayna, that you'd love for me to say it has to be paranormal, but it really could just be some elaborate pranks by local kids, ya know?"

"I know," she admitted, "but it seems like it'd be pretty hard to hit the roof with rocks without being seen every single time."

"Hard, but not impossible." He rubbed his eyes. "I imagine that's the same thing the deputies that took her reports told her."

"Basically, yes."

"Well, there ya go. They would have had a look at the place and a better idea than me – having not seen it – how or where some kids might be able to scurry out of sight after causing trouble."

Rayna shook her head. "I was there, and I really didn't see any good, easy place to be completely out of site and still within throwing distance, unless they had a good arm, great aim, and were brave enough to stand in the creepiest barn I've ever been in."

"Maybe you're dealing with the next Peyton Manning?"

Rayna laughed. "Maybe."

"So, I take it you think there's more to it than kids up to no good?"

"Yes, I actually witnessed something... not normal... inside the house."

The deputy chuckled. "You mean paranormal? You know we all know you around here. You don't have to dance around it." He gave her a quick wink. "What did you see?"

Rayna decided to humor him since he was trying to be helpful. "I saw a ghost!"

"No, way!"

"Way! It was about this tall," Rayna held her hand a little more than chest high, "and basically just a shadow that darted through the room next to the one I was standing in."

"It was probably just a trick of light from a car passing."

"Nope. She had the curtains drawn to keep the heat in."

He tilted his head and thought. "Imagination?"

"Not likely. I was in a focused conversation with the homeowner."

"Day drinking?"

Rayna laughed out loud. "Ha-ha! No, sir! I thought you said you know me around here!"

He grinned. "I had to ask."

"Right," she agreed. "There was other activity while we were there. We all witnessed a marble that doesn't want to stay where it's put – in a closed drawer of a desk in an otherwise empty room."

"Wait. What?"

"Other than the homeowner, Sam, and me, the house was empty, and that room was nearly devoid of furniture, and this marble dropped and rolled on the floor and under the desk. We heard it from the living room, immediately went to investigate the sound, and we found it. She swore she had closed it in the drawer of that desk. We checked, and there were no holes in the drawer."

"Does she have a pet?"

"No."

His brow furrowed. "Hm."

Rayna decided she might as well continue since he was so interested in the story. "So, I borrowed the marble and took it home, and you'll never guess what happened."

"It fell out of your desk, too?"

"No, I had it in a bowl with my keys near my front door. But it did somehow end up on the floor, where my cat chased it, and then ran scared from it."

He smirked. "Cats."

"No, seriously! She chased it down the hall, and something scared the mess out of her."

"What was it?"

"I have no idea."

"Were you scared?"

Rayna paused. "Scared isn't a word I like to use, but it did increase my anxiety level a bit."

"You were scared." He pointed and winked again.

"Startled. I was startled."

"What did you do?"

"I found the marble and told whatever was attached to get out of my house."

"Did you throw the marble out of the house?"

"No, I'm giving it back to her this weekend, so losing it, or tossing it, isn't an option."

"What if the marble is the cause of her problems?"

"I've considered that, but an inanimate object isn't an entity. It's a symbol or a tool or…"

"… Or it's possessed. Wasn't there a cable show about that? Possessed items?"

"Yes, but I don't put a lot of stock in that. The stories are usually more nuanced than they can explain in a TV show."

"Oh." He scratched at his bearded chin. "Who uses a marble for a tool?"

"Good question. I think I know what I'm researching when I get home."

He grinned. "Let me know what you find out." He stood up and straightened his tie and shirt sleeves. "I've got to get moving."

"Thanks for being a sounding board." Rayna said as she took the hint and turned to go.

"My pleasure. Stay warm!"

As Rayna headed toward the door, she paused at Barb's desk and whispered, "Um, what's his name?"

"Who?" Barb looked around.

"The deputy I was just talking with."

"Oh, that's Ray. Don't you know all their names by now?" Barb teased quietly.

"I suck at names, but since we spoke, I'll try to remember next time."

"You should. I think he's sweet on you."

Rayna rolled her eyes and waved goodbye to her friend as she headed toward the door.

Back in her warm home office, Rayna followed Google suggestions down rabbit hole after rabbit hole until she finally found some useful information on a website on the history of witchcraft and folk magic in the South. As many books as she owned on a variety of paranormal topics, witchery was one topic she'd always shied away from. Maybe it was her Catholic upbringing or the fact that the people she'd met in her younger years who claimed to be witches usually seemed to be hung up more on trying to creep people out than actually practicing anything of substance, but the subject always seemed something she'd never have to deal with – at least, until that moment anyway.

Now, she was reading about witch bottles and gris-gris bags and good magic to use against dark magic and how the practice in the southern United States was a mix of neo-paganism, African, and Caribbean rituals, and a little bit of everything else including German folk remedies. Like the rest of American culture, old traditions and new-age rituals bubbled in a melting pot of religion and folklore with just a little unproven "science" thrown in to make it all somehow sound legitimate.

As a scientist, it should have made her chuckle to think about the superstitions that permeated the countryside. As an empath and investigator, it intrigued her. Whether they talked about it or not, most people in her world had at least a few family stories of unexplainable experiences, strange encounters with people who seemed to emit dark energy, or people who appeared to be cursed by bad luck. Some people would avoid walking under ladders, panic over a broken mirror, or freak out at the sighting of a black cat. Not Rayna, of course. Her midnight-colored kitty was her favorite good luck charm, and she knew that most popular superstitions have a logical rationale behind them that's been lost over the centuries while they've been passed down through generations.

But Rayna could see the irony in her natural reaction of scoffing at those old wives' tales and the fact that she was Catholic. Many would point at her beliefs and say she was the pot calling the kettle black, and from their perspective, they'd be right. So, who was she to consider anyone else's spiritual beliefs wrong? She shrugged as she thought about it all.

If there was one thing her experience as an intuitive had taught her, it was to keep an open mind, especially when investigating a case unlike one she'd ever looked into before. And there she was, knee-deep in possible explanations for a marble with a spirit attachment, wondering if it had always been a solo item, or if maybe it had been part of a hex bag. If so, was the hex bag for cursing someone, or was it for protection against the type of person who would create a curse? She'd have to save those questions for Mandy and hope the homeowner had some ideas.

Rayna's phone alerted her to a text. Sam was finally confirming his availability for Saturday's investigation. "Is Wolf coming?" He asked.

"I don't think he'll be home by then. He should be driving back that day," she replied.

"K," was his only response.

Chapter 6

Saturday morning arrived with another burst of Arctic air, but this time there were snow clouds involved. Rayna did her best to psyche herself up for spending the day in a cold house and an even colder barn. The fresh snow would at least help show footprints – or the lack thereof – in the case they had activity that could be blamed on local kids with nothing better to do.

After charging her digital voice recorder and video camera batteries, she texted Mandy that she was on her way to meet the team and head over. Mandy was excited to welcome them back to her home. She said the air there had felt even more unsettled than before Rayna and Sam had visited. Rayna hoped that boded well for finding some answers.

She drove to Sam's house and let him drive to Mandy's. His vehicle had all-wheel drive and was newer than hers or Barb's. Plus, being a passenger for the last stretch of the trip allowed Rayna to do a quick meditation in the back seat in preparation for whatever they might face at Mandy's. She felt the marble resting in her pocket under layers of fleece, and it still felt colder than she expected it to. She was looking forward to handing it back to Mandy, but she couldn't decide whether she should explain how it had misbehaved at her own home.

When they pulled into Mandy's driveway, Rayna noted a second car behind Mandy's and wondered if she'd invited an audience to watch the investigators do their thing. It wouldn't be the first time they worked in front of an audience, but it wasn't something she'd ever get used to. To her relief, the 40-something year-old woman who greeted them at the door immediately introduced herself as Mandy's daughter, Kendra.

Kendra was taller than Mandy with friendly brown eyes and a warm smile. She was dressed for the cold with a thick, wool sweater over a turtleneck and fleece-lined boots. "Come on in," she said, as she held the door open for the trio. "Mom's in the kitchen making some hot coffee for you."

The house was warmer than Rayna remembered it being on their last visit, but still chillier than she was used to. There was a big fire in the fireplace and space heaters scattered about. "Thank you, Mandy!" Rayna called toward the kitchen. She held her still-gloved hand out to Kendra. "It's nice to meet you. This is Sam and Barb." Each gave Kendra a friendly handshake.

Kendra motioned for them to sit down. "Please, make yourselves at home. I'm just here for emotional support for Mom."

Sam sank into the couch and then momentarily struggled to regain his upright posture. "That's kind of you. I hope she isn't worried this will be a stressful visit."

"I think she just wants to get some answers, but she's worried what she learns might be stressful," Kendra said quietly. She looked back toward the kitchen to ensure Mandy was out of earshot. "She was kicked out of her church over this, and she's afraid it might be demonic."

Sam nodded knowingly, Barb let out a little gasp, and Rayna grimaced.

Barb whispered, "Why would they kick her out of church?"

"Because the pastor is one that preaches that anything ghostly is demonic and something a person brings upon themselves by sinning greatly," Kendra answered.

Rayna looked down at her lap and sighed. She hated hearing that news, but it wasn't the first time she'd heard of it happening. "That's a cop out," she finally said.

Kendra smiled knowingly. "That's what I told mom. The pastor is a chicken." There was almost a hint of laughter in her voice. "But she didn't want to hear me talk bad about him. She's been going to that church for years, and she thought pretty highly of him until this."

"That's too bad," Sam said.

"Yeah," Barb agreed.

"I'd like to give pastors like him a piece of my mind," Rayna said, a touch of real anger in her voice.

Kendra leaned toward Rayna and whispered loudly, "I'll give you his number."

Rayna immediately regretted what she'd said, and had no idea why her next words were, "Please do."

Mandy entered the room with an antique silver tray topped with a carafe of coffee, a pitcher of cream, and mugs. "I thought you could use something warm to drink," she said.

Rayna noticed bags under Mandy's eyes as she set the tray on the coffee table between them. "It's nice to see you again, Mandy. Are you feeling well?"

Mandy sat in her chair with a little groan. "I'm fine," she answered. "I just haven't been sleeping well."

"Can I ask why?" Sam inquired.

Mandy nodded. "This place has been noisy since your last visit. Every night at 3:00 AM, something bangs in that room," she pointed to the mostly empty second bedroom. It's like knocking on the walls and sometimes the floor and sometimes the ceiling. It wakes me up at night."

"Every night?" Sam repeated.

"Yes."

The conversation reminded Rayna of the marble in her pocket, so she pulled it out and showed it to Mandy. "Maybe someone is looking for this?" She asked.

Mandy squinted her eyes and recognized the little ball. "Maybe. I hadn't thought of that." She leaned toward Rayna with her hand held out. "May I put it back in the desk?"

"Absolutely!" Rayna answered, a little more eagerly than she meant to.

"Thank you," Mandy took it and immediately walked to the back bedroom to put it away.

Kendra watched quietly as each of the trio poured themselves a cup of coffee. "So, how does this work?" She finally asked.

"An investigation?" Rayna asked.

"Yes. How does your investigation work?"

Sam took the lead, "Well, first we'll set up Rayna's video camera wherever she thinks it will do the most good. Then, we'll do about a 15-minute EVP session in each room inside the house. Then, we'll go do one in the barn."

"EVP?" Kendra asked.

Sam replied, "That stands for electronic voice phenomena. You see, we use these digital voice recorders," he pulled his small device out of his pocket and held it up for her to see, "to record question and answer sessions in each room. We ask questions and wait quietly for answers. Usually, that means just sitting in silence for about 30 seconds after each question and then asking another. Then we take the recordings home and listen to see if we hear answers from anyone not physically present in the room."

Kendra's eyes narrowed as she thought about it. "You mean like a ghost?"

"Basically, yes," Sam answered.

"And do you ever get those answers?" Kendra asked him.

"Sometimes."

Mandy spoke up as she reentered the living room. "What do ghosts sound like?"

Rayna answered before Sam could. "They often sound like people who are whispering, which is why when we do this, we ask that nobody whispers. Use your normal voices, so we don't mistake you for a ghost." She winked at Mandy, who understood.

"Yes, ma'am," Mandy replied. "Really like people? They don't growl or … or anything like that?"

"Sometimes we get growls," Barb answered.

Kendra shook her head. "I don't think I'd like that."

"It's not fun to listen to," Sam assured her.

Rayna could see the discussion going in a darker direction, so she piped in. "Usually, we hear whispers. Occasionally, we hear voices that are just as loud as everyone else in the room, but not matching any of us. Rarely, we'll get something that could be construed as a growl. I mean very, very rarely. We're hoping to hear answers that make sense to the questions so that we can pinpoint who might be hanging out in your house. If we can learn that, we can work to send them on their way to the other side."

"You mean heaven," Kendra asked.

"You could say that," Rayna answered. "I hope to send them into the light and then let whoever greets them on the other side sort out exactly where they should be."

Mandy gave a little laugh at that answer. "According to my pastor, it will be hell."

"I'm not the judge or jury in the case, so it's not up to me, or us," Rayna replied. "I've heard of men like your pastor, Mandy. I don't think he's the best one to decide either."

"What do you mean?" Mandy asked.

"I mean that if you went to him for help about this and his response was to ask you to leave the church and turn his back on you, he's not one that should be judging anybody's soul."

Kendra nodded, "I told her that."

Mandy said, "He's a good man."

Sam shot Rayna a look that told her to change the subject, so she did. "Anyway, we're going to spend just an hour or two here if that's okay. Then we'll go home and review our recordings and let you know if we capture anything."

"That sounds good to me. Do you want us to just stay here in the living room?" Mandy asked.

Rayna answered, "That's totally up to you."

Mandy looked at Kendra, who gave her a reassuring nod. Then, she looked around the house and shrugged. "We'll just sit here and be quiet. I don't need to follow you around."

Rayna nodded knowingly. "You'll be able to hear us while we're inside anyway, and I'm sure you'd rather not visit the barn, right?"

Mandy let out a slight gasp. "You read my mind!"

"Nah," Rayna replied, "it just makes sense."

They finished their coffee, each lost in their own thoughts for the moment. Then Rayna retrieved her video camera from its bag and walked into the kitchen. "I'm going to set this up about where I was standing when I saw your visitor last time, if that's okay, Mandy."

"You mean the ghost?" Mandy called to her.

"If that's what you want to call it, yes. I'm pointing the camera back toward the living room."

"Okay," Mandy confirmed. "I'll be sure not to move."

Sam couldn't stifle his chuckle. "It's okay to move, ma'am. We're just letting you know that if you get up and do a little dance, you'll be on video."

Kendra giggled and Mandy nodded. Barb stood up and walked around the living room, glancing around at the walls and the doorways. "There's not a lot of light coming in from outside, is there?"

Mandy shook her head. "I keep the thermal curtains on the windows this time of year to try to keep the heat in. Is that a problem for the video?"

"No, ma'am. I'm just observing in case we do see anything on video."

Satisfied that the camera was placed properly, Rayna rejoined the group in the living room. "Are you ready to get started?"

Everyone nodded in agreement, and Kendra reached over and patted Mandy on the leg. "You okay, Mom?"

"I'm fine," she answered. "Let's get this rolling."

Sam, Barb, and Rayna all put their voice recorders in different areas of the room. Sam set his on the coffee table, Rayna put hers on the mantle, and Barb placed hers on an end table. Then Rayna started the session. "EVP session number one. We're going to go around the room and introduce ourselves. I'm Rayna."

"I'm Barb."

"I'm Sam."

"I'm Kendra."

"I'm Mandy."

Rayna asked, "Is there anyone else here who wants to introduce themselves?"

Then they waited in silence.

Rayna could feel Mandy's anxiety rising as they took turns asking questions like "who are you," "why are you here," and "do you have anything to do with the barn or the cemetery?" After about fifteen minutes, she announced the session was over. "What do you think?" she asked as she turned off her voice recorder.

"I think I hope you get some answers," Mandy answered. "I'm just worried if you do, they won't be nice."

"It will be okay, no matter what we find, Mandy," Rayna replied. "I'm not going to leave you to deal with this by yourself anymore."

As Sam, Barb, and Rayna took their recorders to Mandy's bedroom for the next session, Sam whispered to Rayna, "How are you so confident?"

Rayna just looked at him and shrugged. "We're going to figure this one out," she answered quietly.

Kendra's voice rang out from the other room, "I thought you said, 'no whispering'!"

Sam laughed. "Yes, we did. I just broke my own rules."

The team repeated their EVP session with a mix of the same and new questions in each room. When they were satisfied that they'd covered all their bases in the house, they excused themselves and headed for the barn.

Outside, Barb asked Rayna, "Did you feel anything in there?"

"Not much other than Mandy's stress. The poor thing seems concerned that bringing us in might have made things worse."

"I got that, too," Barb said. They walked momentarily in silence, listening to their boots crunch the fresh snow on the way to the barn. As they got closer to its doors, Barb slowed her pace. "We're going in there?"

"Yes," Rayna answered. "Why?"

"I'm no psychic, but I don't like the feeling I'm getting."

"Join the club," Rayna answered. She looked at her friend and realized Barb was genuinely spooked. "You don't have to go in if you don't want to," she told her. "It's totally fine to go back inside that warm… er house."

Barb gave herself a little hug and looked back and forth between Sam and Rayna, considering the option. "No," she finally said. "I'm coming, but I'm standing between you two the whole time."

Sam put his arm around Barb's shoulders. "I got ya," he reassured her.

Rayna pulled the barn door open. She expected the daylight to illuminate the opening, but it felt as though the darkness spilled out toward them. Barb took a half-step backwards.

"It's okay," Rayna said, not completely convinced herself but trying to sound confident for her friends.

"Let's do this," she said dramatically as she pushed the red button on her voice recorder and its LED lit up. Sam and Barb nodded and did the same. Then, almost as a single unit, the three walked inside together.

The air inside was warmer than they expected. Really warm. Rayna took her flashlight out of her pocket and used it to scan the space for a source for the heat. "Do you feel that?"

"What?" Barb asked in an unsteady voice.

"How warm it is in here."

"Yeah," Sam answered. "Should it be this warm?"

"I don't know," Rayna answered and stepped away from them to further inspect the barn. "I don't see any reason it shouldn't be as cold as it was last time. There are no space heaters or anything."

"I'm not even sure there's electricity out here. I don't see any outlets," Sam said as he swept his own flashlight beam along the walls.

Barb's voice was nearly a whisper when she spoke. "Y'all, I'm really not feeling well." She stepped closer to Sam and leaned on him. "I think I'm going to be sick."

Rayna shined her light toward her friends, and Barb's skin was almost gray. "Take her outside," she said to Sam. He nodded and guided Barb to the doorway. When he reached the daylight near the entry, he turned to see that Rayna hadn't moved from the darkness. "You coming?"

"No."

"We're supposed to use the buddy system, remember? I can't keep an eye on both of you."

Rayna shined the light toward her own face, "I'm fine. Take her out. Get her some air." Sam just stood there staring at her for a moment, so she added, "It's just a barn."

Sam finally nodded and guided Barb outside. Rayna stood still while she watched the shadows of her friends move out of view. She took a deep breath through her nose and let it out slowly to calm her nerves. Then she did something reflexively that she hadn't done in a very long time. She used her right hand to make the sign of the cross from her forehead to her heart to her left shoulder, and then to her right shoulder. Instantly, a chill passed through her, reminding her of something her mother used to say: *when you get a quick shiver like that it means an angel just walked over your grave.*

"No," she said aloud. "What does that even mean?" Then, she steeled her nerves more and said, "Lord, protect me. It's just a barn, right?"

For a brief moment, a low noise emanated from the far corner of the barn, and she quickly shone her flashlight in that direction. There was nothing there. It was the single empty corner in the whole place, and it didn't make sense. Before she could convince herself the sound was her imagination, it happened again, from the same area, but louder. It was clearly a growl this time – almost like you'd expect from a big dog.

She stood there facing the sound, but there was no living thing in front of her. She glanced down at the voice recorder in her gloved hand. It was on, and she hoped it picked up the sound. Slowly she took a few steps toward that corner, and then there was silence. Reminding herself to breathe, she took another step in that direction. This time the growl was louder and right in front of her. She could feel a puff of hot breath on her face and the smell of something rotten made her nearly wretch. Without a thought, she backed up a few steps. "Sam?" She called weakly, but there was no answer. When she felt another puff of hot air hit her, Rayna realized her options were to face off with some invisible, growling entity or forsake her dignity and leave the barn. Careful not to run because she felt like whatever was there was predatory, she backed up a few more steps, turned toward the doors, and walked as casually as she could force herself toward them, all the while feeling that familiar pressure on her back of some unseen presence staring angrily at her.

The feeling took her back to her childhood, a time before she understood the sensation. She'd walk into a place with paranormal activity and get an intense pressure in the center of her back, and fight or flight would kick in. Back then, she ran. Now, she knew better. As she reached the exit, she said with all the strength she could muster, "You must stay in the barn. You cannot follow us anywhere!" After a few more steps, she glanced behind her and noticed the pressure sensation was fading. After two more steps, she broke into a sprint. Noticing Sam and Barb's tracks in the snow, she followed them to the front of the house and was relieved to see Barb leaning on Mandy's front door, the color back in her face.

"What happened?" Sam said as Rayna slowed to a walk. "I haven't seen you run in... well, I don't know when the last time I saw you run was."

Rayna realized the recorder was still in her hand and hit the stop button. "I hope I got it."

"Got what?" Barb asked.

Rayna looked at her intently and asked, "Are you okay?"

"Yes," she answered. "I'm fine. I felt better as soon as we got over here. I'm just taking a breath. Got what?"

"There's something nasty in that barn. Angry. Smells of rot and..." Rayna couldn't finish her sentence because her mind was racing.

"And?" Sam and Barb asked in unison.

"I need a priest."

Chapter 7

Sam's A-frame house felt safe and warm. For being the home of a confirmed bachelor, it was decorated tastefully and always reminded Rayna of what she'd expect to see in the Alps. He loved the architectural style and ran with it when choosing furnishings and accents. Not long after he bought it, she asked him if he just took a magazine photo to a designer and asked for help getting the look. He didn't give a straight answer but told her that if was going to live in a home full of windows, he wanted to ensure people outside looking in didn't think he was a slob.

Rayna barely spoke all the way back to Sam's house from Mandy's. She sat in the back seat silently with her eyes closed, her mind still reeling from her experience in the barn. She thought through all the possibilities and wondered what other explanations could be out there that she wasn't even aware of, yet. When they arrived at Sam's, she followed them inside, sat down at his dining table and just stared at the dark wooden top. The natural shapes imprinted in the wood reminded her of faces and eyes. *Pareidolia*, she thought. The brain looks for familiar images even in chaos. Yet, there was nothing but darkness in her mind's eye when she tried to put a face on the entity in the barn.

Sam finally broke the silence as he and Barb joined her at the table. "Rayna, you've got us worried. I've never seen you shaken up like this. Just tell us what happened."

"Yeah, please tell us," Barb urged.

Rayna sighed. "I've been going over it in my head trying to explain it, or at least rationalize it," she finally looked each of her friends in the eyes. "There's nothing mundane about it."

"What was it?" Sam pleaded.

"Okay," Rayna nodded her head, assuring herself that her friends would believe her. "When you left, something growled at me."

"Growled?" Barb repeated?

"Yes, at first it sounded like it was in the corner farthest from the doors. So, I looked in that direction, expecting an animal like a dog or something, but there wasn't anything there. So, I thought I'd check it out, and it growled again from the same direction, but closer. While I was trying to figure it out, or when I was trying to figure it out. I mean what it could be…" she wasn't sure how to describe it.

"Yes?" Sam asked when she trailed off. "Rayna, just spit it out."

"It was right in my face when it growled again." She raised her hand, palm flat two inches from her own nose. "It was right here, and its breath was so rank that I almost hurled."

"You saw it?" Barb asked.

"No! That's the problem. I never saw it, but it was right in front of me. It was angry and growling, and I've never felt that kind of fear in my life." That was it. She finally admitted it to Sam and Barb and to herself. She had been terrified, and she wasn't used to that feeling. "I'm ashamed to say I got the hell out of there as fast as I could go without looking like out-and-out prey."

"No kidding!" Sam reached over and patted her on the shoulder. "I think anyone would have had the same reaction, but most people would have just run like hell!"

"I wanted to, but my nature training kicked in, so I walked until I was sure it couldn't leave the barn."

Barb asked, "How could you tell it couldn't leave the barn?"

"The feeling of its presence," she pointed to her own back. "You know, that feeling I get? It faded when I was several steps past the doors. Then, I ran."

Sam nodded at her reassuringly. "So, when you told us you hoped you got it, that *it* was the growling?"

"Yes."

"Where's your recorder?" He asked.

Rayna pulled her voice recorder out of her pocket. "Right here."

He grinned. "Ladies, I say we order a pizza and have an EVP listening party."

"I could eat," Barb said, and she reached into her pocket, pulled her little silver recorder out, and set it on the table.

Sam did the same. "Pepperoni and mushrooms?"

"Works for me!" Barb replied.

"Sure," Rayna answered with less enthusiasm.

"No mushrooms?" Sam asked.

Rayna shook her head. "No, pepperoni and mushrooms are fine. I'm just not in a hurry to hear that growl again."

"Oh!" Barb excitedly tapped her hands on the table. "I have an idea! Let's exchange recorders. That way you don't have to listen to it, but we can still see if it's there."

Rayna said nothing and slid her voice recorder across the table to Barb while Sam pulled his phone out of his other pocket and dialed Rocco's Pizza on Main.

"Do you need headphones?" Barb asked.

"They're in my bag," Rayna told her.

Once the pizza was ordered, all three were sitting at the table with headphones on, listening to their EVP sessions. Barb skipped past a couple of the house files to get to the barn audio quickly, and Rayna didn't have to guess when Barb heard the growl because she jumped, pushed the chair from the table, and took her headphones off – all in one swift motion.

"Wow!" Barb said, with her hand to her chest. "You weren't kidding."

Rayna nodded. "It's there?"

"Oh, it's there! And that's no dog. That was… guttural. I mean seriously! How did you not run?"

"Did you hear all three?" Rayna asked.

"Oh, wait. That's right. You said there were three. That was just the first one, I guess." Barb picked up her headphones and put them back on. She hit rewind on the recorder to go back to her stopping point and listened some more. Her eyes widened at the second one, and when she heard the third one, she ripped the headphones back off her head and handed the recorder to Sam. "You listen."

Sam took the headphones from Barb and replaced his with them. Barb rewound the file and hit "play." Both women watched Sam's face as he listened intently, but he did his best to keep a poker face until the last one. "Holy crap! That was loud!"

"And rage-filled!" Barb added.

"Yeah," Sam agreed. "How did you not run? I would have run, and I don't ever run."

Their reactions made Rayna feel better about her own. "I just knew that would be a bad idea."

Sam took the recorder from Barb and listened to the recording a few more times. Satisfied that he'd heard all there was to hear, he took the headphones off and looked at Rayna with admiration. "My dear, you are possibly the bravest person I know."

Rayna scoffed. "I was terrified."

"And yet, you kept your head."

She shrugged. "Like I said, I just knew running could be a trigger for something worse to happen."

Barb asked, "So, what do y'all think that thing is?"

Rayna shrugged again and rested her chin in her hands as she leaned forward. "I hate to say what it could be."

Sam leaned back in his chair. "If you hate to say it, then I will. Rage-filled growl, exceptional heat, rotting odor – all point to one thing in my book. Might be a demon."

Barb shook her head and looked at Rayna, "I was afraid you'd say that."

Rayna straightened her posture, "I didn't say it." She pointed at Sam. "I'm not ready to say it."

"What else could it be?" Sam asked earnestly.

"I think there are other options," Rayna answered. "I just need to figure out what those are. In the meantime, let's go through the rest of the audio and see if we got anything in the house, okay?"

After about an hour and most of a large pizza, they had two more interesting audio clips from Mandy's house. One was a single-syllable answer to a yes-or-no question that sounded like a "yes" in response to "Was the red marble yours?" The second one sounded like a partial answer to "What's your name?"

"So, what are our next steps?" Sam asked as he took the dirty dishes from the table.

"We have to tell Mandy what we found, don't we?" Barb asked.

"Yes," Rayna answered, "but first I want to do a little more research. You know the last thing I ever want to tell the poor woman is that she has a demon in her barn."

"So, to the library next?" Sam asked.

"You can go to the library and see if you can find any history on the property, or even look in the paper's archives," Rayna told him. "Barb, can you look up property in another county to see the list of owners?"

"Yes," she answered. "I should be able to access the tax records."

"Good," Rayna nodded.

Sam asked, "What are you going to do?"

"Tomorrow's Sunday, right?"

"Yes," he answered.

"I'm going to church."

"Oh, that reminds me," he said, pulling a piece of paper out of his back pocket and handing it to Rayna, "Kendra asked me to give this to you while you were sitting in the car. While we were outside, she made an appointment for you to meet Mandy's pastor."

Rayna's heart sank. "She did what?"

"You probably shouldn't have offered to give him a piece of your mind."

Chapter 8

Sunday morning's sunrise revealed a few more inches of fresh snow in Rayna's yard. She heard the county's plows moving through town, scraping away any excuse she had to change her mind about going to church. It wasn't that she dreaded it, though. She had just gotten out of the habit of going and the idea seemed foreign to her now. She was amazed at how easily she could break a good habit compared to breaking bad habits like eating too many sweets.

As she stared out of her kitchen window waiting for the coffee to finish brewing, her phone alerted her to a text. "I'll be home on Tuesday, and I can't wait to see you," Wolf sent. Her mood instantly improved.

"Wonderful!" She replied, and then added, "If you'd like, I'll cook you dinner."

"More wonderful!" He texted back.

Wolf's text reminded Rayna that she needed to tell her mother he'd be missing Sunday dinner. With all her activities, Rayna had forgotten to text her mom about it. She typed a quick message to let her know, and by the time Rayna poured her coffee, her mother had replied that it was fine. Her sister and the kids had to postpone anyway, so dinner was moved to next Sunday.

"Great!" Rayna replied, thankful that sarcasm was hard to read through typed words.

Mass was as she remembered it. Of course, growing up Catholic meant the stories didn't change much from year to year, but the homily – the priest's message after the readings – would be different depending on the week. She recognized Father Martin Connor, a middle-aged man with streaks of gray in his curly red hair, as he entered the church when mass began. He had been one of her favorite priests because he seemed to have a quiet wisdom about him and always seemed to be speaking directly to her during his homilies. Other parishioners had said the same.

Rayna stayed seated after mass as everyone else filed out. She sat and wondered if Father Martin would notice her there, or if she should catch his attention to ask him her questions. Even after all her thought, she still wasn't sure exactly what to ask him. Parish priests rarely had experience with the paranormal as far as she knew, and she wasn't sure how he'd feel about the subject.

When just a couple other church members were left scattered about the sanctuary, seemingly lost in prayer, she looked toward the exit and saw the priest looking back at her. She motioned to him that she'd like to speak to him, and he nodded.

Sitting down next to her, he said quietly, "Hi, Rayna, welcome back."

"Hi, Father. Thank you," she replied.

"How have you been?"

"I've been pretty well – just working a lot and being admittedly lazy on Sundays. I'm trying to do better."

"Well, being here today is a great start." He smiled.

"Yesterday was a rough day," she told him, still unsure exactly how to broach the subject.

"How so?"

She looked down at her hands and took a deep breath. "I have this client," she started.

"A weather client?"

"Um, no. A paranormal client." She looked at him to gauge his response, and to her surprise his face showed no shock, so she continued. "She's a sweet, older lady in Vickerton, and she asked my group to help her with some activity in her house and her barn." It helped Rayna to remember that the whole town knew her avocation after last summer's adventures, even if they didn't truly know every detail.

"And you did that yesterday?"

"Yes, we investigated yesterday."

"What did you find?"

"I'm pretty sure what's in the house is a human spirit. I'm still not quite sure why it's there, but we're working on research that might help us figure that out."

"And the barn? Is it the ghost of a horse or something?"

"I wish."

The priest cocked his head like a confused puppy. "You wish?"

Rayna shook her head, "No, I don't really mean that. I just mean what's in the barn doesn't seem that mundane."

"So, what do you mean?"

Rayna told Father Martin her experience. Her voice shook a little as she explained how frightened she was in the moment, and he listened intently when she explained the growls were on the voice recorder, so they couldn't have been imagined.

He broke his gaze on her and looked toward the altar. "I see," he said and then paused for a moment. "What do you think that was?"

Rayna laughed quietly. "I was hoping you could tell me."

"A demon?" He asked.

"I'm not sure that it's that simple. I mean, not that a demon is simple, but it seems like that would be a straight-forward answer. Despite the signs, I feel like there's more to it, but it's something I..." She searched for the right words. "Maybe it's something I'm not yet aware of." She paused. "Do you think it's a demon?"

The priest kept his gaze on the altar for another moment and then looked at her with a slight smile. "I certainly hope it isn't."

"Same here," she sighed.

"Look," he said, "it takes courage to face the unknown and to try to help a stranger with an issue like this. Maybe not everyone would see it this way, but you're doing the Lord's work."

Rayna nodded in understanding. "I'm glad you think so. I didn't know who else to talk to about something like this."

"I'm afraid I don't have a lot of experience in anything paranormal beyond what happens when people cross over." Rayna's eyes grew bigger with interest at that statement, but Father Martin shook his head. "Those are stories for another day."

"Okay. I'm going to hold you to that," she told him.

"I'll ask a few of the other priests I know that have had some dealings with darker things what they think. Is your number the same as what's in the parish directory?"

"Yes."

"I'll let you know if they have anything helpful for you. In the meantime, I'll ask you to pray for the spirit in the home, and I'll pray as well."

"You will?"

"Yes, of course!"

Rayna's face showed confusion, and she finally asked sheepishly, "Why?"

Father Martin had patience in his voice when he answered, "It's our duty to help those who have passed cross over. It's our responsibility to pray for the repose of their souls so they may rest in peace and eventually gain entry to heaven. That's what All Souls Day is all about, right?"

Rayna nodded, "Oh, yes, that's right. But this one isn't even in Purgatory, yet right? I mean she's wandering around my client's home, so she must not have crossed to anywhere, yet."

"That seems to be the case, but prayers can still help. You can keep it simple or say a Rosary for her. You did say *her*, right?"

Rayna hadn't even realized that she'd said it, but it sounded right. "Yes, I guess I feel like it's female."

"Well, then you could be one step closer to an identity, but you can pray for her with or without a name. All you need is good intention." He stood to leave and pointed toward a woman sitting near rows of votive candles along a wall. "Now, if you'll excuse me, I think she also needs my prayers."

"Yes, Father," Rayna said. "Thank you for your time."

"My pleasure, Rayna. I'll be in touch with anything I learn."

Rayna drove from the Catholic church in Jupiter to the small chapel in Vickerton that Mandy used to attend, and once again, the roads had been cleared. No excuses. She had to follow through on her conversation with Kendra. The thought of some so-called man of God throwing a woman out of his church because she asked for help infuriated Rayna, and the closer she got to the chapel, the more things crossed her mind to say to him – most of them weren't kind. So, she reminded herself that you catch more flies with honey and asked God for the right words to show the man he'd made a mistake.

Kendra was waiting for her on the steps of the church. It was the typical small, white country chapel that dot the hillsides of the mountains throughout the region. Rayna wasn't even sure if it was associated with any official denomination, but she'd heard stories of preachers like this one, and she'd met people who had suffered the same religious fate as Mandy.

"I really appreciate you doing this," Kendra told her as she walked up to the church doors. "He's inside. The congregation left a little while ago, so you should be able to talk freely."

"Thanks," Rayna said with a lump in her throat. She cleared it and slowly breathed in the frigid winter air before walking inside. The chapel seemed smaller inside than it looked from the outside. It was dimly lit with a little natural light spilling in from the leaded glass windows that ran along each side. From the doorway, she could see the outline of a man standing near the pulpit on a raised platform at the end of the aisle in front of her. There was an old upright piano to his right, and a small altar to his left. It was a very humble place, and Rayna could see how it could be appealing to Mandy.

Kendra led the way down the aisle toward the pastor. "Pastor Sapp, this is my mom's friend, Rayna, that I told you about. Mom wanted the two of you to meet." Kendra turned to Rayna as she stopped in front of the platform, "Rayna Smith, this is Pastor Richard Sapp."

Rayna thought to herself *honey*, as she held out her gloved hand to shake his. "It's nice to meet you, sir."

He gave her a quick but firm handshake. "To what do I owe this pleasure?" He asked in the tone of a practiced Southern minister. Now that she was closer to him, she could see his features better. He was darker skinned with deep brown eyes, a round face, and a neatly trimmed goatee. He looked friendly enough, but there was an edge to those eyes as he measured her.

"Sir, I'd like to talk with you on behalf of Miss Mandy." Rayna said as politely as she could.

Kendra took a step back from the two of them, and said, "Now that I've made the introductions, I must be on my way. I have to make sure my kids are doing their homework." Then she turned and left them in the dim light of the old church.

"What would you like to talk about?" The pastor asked. Rayna noticed that he stayed on the platform and did not motion that she should take a seat or join him on his level. He just stood there, two steps above her, looking down at her.

"Sir," Rayna started as she moved up one step closer to his level. "Mandy tells me that she came to you for help with a situation she is dealing with in her home."

"Are you referring to something of the... say... ghostly variety?"

"Yes, I am."

He nodded, still looking down at her. "Go on." Now the edge was in his voice.

"She told me that when she asked you for help, you kicked her out of your church, and worse, your congregation. Is that true?"

"It is."

"I have to ask why you would do that."

The pastor sighed dramatically. "Because any woman associating with demons does not belong in my church." He gestured to the pews and added, "I have souls to save, and she would threaten my work."

"Threaten?" Rayna heard the truth that he didn't mean to speak.

"Rayna Smith, is it? I've heard of you. You and your friends are worse than she is."

"Excuse me? How so?" Rayna shoved her hands in her coat pockets to hide the fists she made reflexively.

"Any souls that aren't in heaven aren't human souls. They're demons and you're fools for associating with them. I don't tolerate fools."

Rayna dropped her gaze as she thought through her response. "Where did you learn that souls not in heaven are demons? I'd like to know so I can better understand."

He picked a black-leather clad, well-worn Bible from the pulpit and raised it over his head. "In this good book, it says so."

"And it says that people who investigate alleged paranormal activity are fools? What does it say about people who are trying to help a sweet woman who is afraid in her own home through no fault of her own?"

"That woman brought this on herself."

"How? By buying a house that she'd loved since her childhood?"

"I don't know what she's done, but she wouldn't be tormented if she weren't a sinner."

Rayna tilted her head and looked at the man intently. She took her hands out of her pockets and raised them, pointed to him and back to herself, "Aren't we all sinners? I mean, that's why God sent his only son to save us, right? Because humans are naturally sinners. By that logic, shouldn't we all be dealing with demonic forces in our homes?"

"What? No." His face was taking on a hint of red as Rayna kept talking.

"Tell me in the Bible where it says we should turn our backs on people who ask us for help. Show me where it says we should ignore cries for mercy or that we should deny a child of God a peaceful existence."

"Don't you lecture me!" He slammed the Bible down on the pulpit and jammed his pointed finger onto it repeatedly. "I am a man of God. How dare you come into my church and question my decisions concerning the health of my flock!"

"Oh, I dare. I dare because I'm a daughter of God. Because I can point to the Book of Tobit and tell you exactly where the Angel prescribes burning incense to cleanse a tormented woman of bad spirits. I can point to the place in the New Testament where Jesus sent his apostles out into the world with the power to cast out demons in his name. And I can point to the Beatitudes that says people like Mandy will get into heaven long before the people that hold themselves higher than her because they think they're so much more righteous than she is." Rayna didn't wait to be asked to leave; she was already turning toward the door as the anger rose in his face and his eyes narrowed. "I'll tell you how I dare. Mandy came to me and my friends for help, and with God's power, we're going to help her because unlike you, we're not cowards."

"Get out!" He bellowed from the platform.

Rayna stopped at the back of the church and spoke from the shadows, "I'll tell you one thing Pastor, there's a difference between using the Bible as a shield and hiding behind it. My friends and I? We don't hide." And with that, she quickly walked out the doors and left the man in his dark little church.

She could feel the heat drain from her face as she started the car. Rayna had never been a fan of confrontations, and she couldn't believe she'd just stood up to another bully on behalf of someone who couldn't. But then, after a lifetime of standing up to people who thought she should bow to them, maybe she was getting used to it.

Back at home, Rayna stared at a wall of books in her bedroom with a nagging feeling that there was something in one of them on the paranormal that she needed to read. Somehow, she knew it wasn't anything she'd read before, but that didn't narrow it down. She had books that she'd read, books she'd read parts of, and books that had been on her to-read list for years. Anytime she found a book with a paranormal, mysterious, mythical, or parapsychological theme, she bought it. And now an entire wall full of those books teased her.

She inhaled deeply, exhaled slowly, and closed her eyes. "Show me what I need to know," she said aloud. Then, she put her hand out toward the shelves and slowly moved it in a circle, hoping to feel some pull toward the right book. Nothing. Occasionally that trick worked, but there was nothing pulling her toward any one direction.

"I know there's something here," she spoke again. "Angels, spirit guides, God, beings of the light… someone up there, please guide me."

There was a thump in the living room. At first, she thought it was Cloud playing with a toy, but one glance toward the door reminded her that Cloud was, in fact, asleep on her bed. Rayna cocked her head to listen. Another thump sounded a few seconds later, so she went to investigate. Nothing was out of place, nobody was at the door, and a glance out the window into the darkness of the early evening told her nobody was near her house. She shrugged it off and went back to her bedroom to stare at the bookshelves again.

As she entered, she was stunned to see a book face-down on the floor in front of one of the shelves. She shot Cloud a curious glance, but the cat hadn't moved. Normally, when Grumpy was active, Cloud would at least take notice. Rayna walked over and cautiously picked up the book to read the cover. *The Witchcraft Encyclopedia* was thick and apparently forgotten. "When did I buy this?" Rayna asked herself. She stood up and looked around the room. When she was sure nothing else was out of place, she simply said, "Thank you, whoever helped me today." Whether her helper had been any of those she'd invoked or Grumpy, it didn't truly matter, but at times like this, it would have been nice to know.

Rayna sat down on her bed and absent-mindedly petted Cloud. The little cat popped her head up and gave her a green-eyed glance before settling into a purr. "Let's see what we have here, shall we?" Rayna said as she flipped to the book open to the table of contents, which wasn't very helpful since it was an Encyclopedia. So, she turned to the index in the back of the book and scanned it for anything that jumped out at her. The first thing was *sigils*. She'd heard of them but flipped to the relevant page and read the two-paragraph entry. Suddenly, the symbols on the barn door made a little more sense.

Rayna's next rabbit hole began with the entry for *elementals*. She'd heard other paranormal investigators toss that word around in very matter of fact ways referring to nonhuman spirits that inhabit the natural world. While elementals are an essential part of some folklore and mythology, Rayna's scientific mind had a hard time believing they could be responsible for modern-day troubles. Still, a few days ago, she didn't think she'd have an invisible entity of some type growl in her face in an extra-warm barn on a cold winter's day. She read on but decided that elemental wasn't quite what she was looking for, but it did remind her of another word she'd heard in passing, *tulpa*.

The word wasn't in the book, so she took the tome to her computer desk in the living room and googled it. According to the articles she read, a tulpa is a thought-form created for a purpose, often for healing or protection. She was pretty sure the thing in the barn wasn't interested in healing or doing anything helpful, at least from her perspective.

That was it! She was looking at it from a victim's perspective. Why would that thing be in the barn in the first place? Maybe it was protecting something someone else treasured – like the tales of dragons protecting gold. The idea had merit, but still didn't feel quite right. How likely was it that there would be buried treasure in a barn on old farmland in eastern Tennessee?

Next Rayna looked up thought-forms, and the more general idea began to make more sense. She called Father Martin to ask what he might know about the subject, but he didn't answer. She left an awkward voicemail and asked him to text her when he had time to chat. Then she went back to thumbing through the encyclopedia.

Chapter 9

Somehow, time on Monday felt like it moved simultaneously slower than a snail's pace and lightning fast. Rayna woke at 5:00 AM and was working her weekday routine – making forecasts, communicating with clients, updating forecasts, writing forecast discussions, scanning weather news for interesting tidbits from other parts of the world – and done with all of it much earlier than usual. By noon, she was staring at the clock on her computer wondering why it wasn't later in the day. After running through the daily task list in her mind for the fifth time, she was finally convinced she hadn't forgotten anything and was actually finished with her work until she needed to create the afternoon forecast updates.

At that point, she let her mind wander back to the barn. She had meant it when she told the preacher that she and her friends would help Mandy no matter how frightening the situation. Besides, if it was scary to her, how bad must it be to live there? The whole reason she started investigating hauntings was to help people feel comfortable in their homes. Nobody should be afraid in their own house. She knew that feeling from childhood, and it was frustration verging on helplessness.

Whatever was in the barn was not the same thing, or person, that was in Mandy's house. The barn was dark, possibly evil, and definitely angry. Rayna hoped that Father Martin, Sam, Barb, or someone could shed some light on it. Finding more information about the history of the house might help. She interrupted her thoughts to text Barb and Sam, "Any luck with Mandy's house history?" and waited a moment before putting her phone back down.

The more Rayna thought about the presence inside Mandy's house, the more she was sure it was feminine and likely a family relation. It meant no harm but was still troublesome to Mandy because she couldn't identify it, and it wanted attention. The question was why. And why now? She'd lived there a while before anything that might be paranormal started happening. Had there been some sort of anniversary or trigger? Was the spirit there to relay a message that was falling on deaf ears, or was there something more? And was it connected to the marble?

Rayna considered texting Mandy to ask if the house had been any quieter since their visit, but she worried the state she'd been in when they left might have caused Mandy some consternation. Maybe it would be better if Sam asked. She picked her phone back up to text him, and it rang in her hand, startling her so much that she almost dropped it.

"Hello?"

"Rayna, this is Father Martin."

"Hi Father, how are you?"

"I'm well, and you?

"I'm doing okay. I'm actually sitting here thinking about the case."

"Oh, good. Good. Then, I called at a good time?"

"Perfect timing," Rayna said with a smile. "Did you find anything out?"

"Actually, I might have learned a little something that could point you in a new direction."

"Really? What?" Rayna felt a twinge of excitement.

"Have you ever heard of a servitor?"

Rayna thought for a moment, scanning the paranormal Rolodex in her brain. "No, I don't think I have."

"I hadn't either, but a priest friend of mine up in Massachusetts has spent some time studying occult practices because, you know, Salem's an interesting place..."

"I can imagine."

"Yes, so he and I talked about your experience and how you were looking for other less obvious possibilities besides a demon, and he thought it could be a servitor."

Since Rayna was sitting at her computer, she quickly googled the term. The Wikipedia.com entry read:

> Within chaos magic, a servitor is a psychological complex, deliberately created by the magician for a specific purpose, that appears to operate autonomously from the magician's consciousness; i.e., as if it were an independently existing being.

"Okay," she said. "I just googled it. So, it's kind of like a tulpa but maybe worse?"

"From what he explained, it could be much worse. Tulpas, I think, tend to have positive purposes, but servitors are generally created to... um... carry out its master's bidding. Gosh! That sounds so fantastical that I can't believe I even said it."

"Welcome to my world, Father," Rayna laughed.

"Thanks," he replied. She could tell he was smiling. "This truly is fascinating."

"Did he happen to say how we could tell if that's what it is, or better yet, how to get rid of it?"

"All he could say is that if that is what the entity is, then you'll need to learn its purpose in order to defeat it."

"Has he had this experience before?"

"I asked, and no. He's only read about it."

Rayna sighed, "Okay. That's more than I knew five minutes ago, so it's definitely helpful."

"I'm sorry I don't have more."

"No, don't be sorry. I'm so grateful for your help! Really! Any information is good!" She paused and then asked, "Do you have any advice for me in dealing with this?"

This time, the priest paused. After a moment, he answered, "Do you know the prayer to Saint Michael?"

Rayna nearly facepalmed herself. "Of course!"

"Use it. It's his job to help us in situations like this, but you have to ask him with a humble heart and deep intent."

"I don't know why that didn't occur to me. I used to say it almost daily when I was younger and hadn't learned how to deal with my paranormal life. It was almost as natural as breathing back then."

"Sometimes, it just takes an outside perspective to remember these things. Would you like to make a confession before you return there? It may help prepare you."

Rayna didn't have to think hard about that one, "Yes, but over the phone?"

Father Martin laughed. "No, ma'am. You need to come down to the church, but I won't make you do it during my regular hours. Just call me and let me know when you're coming."

"Thank you, Father. I appreciate it."

"You're welcome. Have a good afternoon."

"You, too."

It had been years since Rayna had even considered the sacrament of reconciliation – an opportunity to lay out all her sins and spiritual shortcomings in front of God and heartily ask for forgiveness. While she didn't feel like she had committed anything egregious, she knew she would need to feel as relieved of that burden as possible before she tackled the thing in the barn.

The phone pinged in her hand with a text message from Sam. "I might have found something of use. Can we meet this evening?"

Almost immediately came a response from Barb, "Just found something, too."

Rayna texted back to the group message, "I'm game. Come on over after my 3pm updates."

The sun was setting as Rayna wrapped up her afternoon forecast updates, but it was only 5 o'clock. Rayna hated winter because it was a season trapped in darkness. So many of her meteorologist cohorts celebrated the chance to forecast snow with all its challenges and excitement, but Rayna wasn't enthusiastic about any of it. She supposed she had seasonal affective disorder but had not bothered to ask about a diagnosis. All she knew was it was a struggle to stay her usual upbeat self when the sun was down before the workday was done.

Headlights refracting through her front window told her that one of her friends was arriving right on time, but the height didn't look right for Barb's or Sam's car. Her heart skipped a beat and confusion clouded her mind as she realized the vehicle pulling into her driveway was Wolf's – a day early, right? She sat frozen in her chair as she told herself it couldn't be him. He'd said Tuesday. She glanced at her phone and thought about checking his text messages to be sure, but there wasn't time. Someone knocked at the kitchen door on the side of her house near the driveway.

As Rayna rose to cross the room, she called out, "Who is it?"

"Sasquatch!" a familiar voice answered, and she ran through the hallway, into the kitchen, and nearly crashed into the kitchen door as her socks slid across the floor. Unlocking and opening it as fast as she could, she threw herself into Wolf's open arms. "You alright?" He asked.

"I'm better now!" She told him as she planted a kiss on him. "Oh, your lips are cold. Come inside!" Rayna stepped back to let him enter. "Why is your face so cold?"

"The heater in my Jeep stopped working about an hour ago," he said as he stepped inside and slid his snow-covered boots off and onto her welcome mat.

"Oh, my gosh! You poor thing!"

"It's okay. I'll get it looked at tomorrow."

"Wait. Weren't you supposed to be here tomorrow? Not today?"

"Do you mind?" He asked with a concerned look on his face. He took his knit cap off and his straight, black hair fell down past his shoulders.

"No, not at all. I was just..."

"Yes, I told you Tuesday, but I couldn't wait, so I came home early."

Rayna hugged him again. "Take that cold jacket off. Let's get you warmed up."

"Yes, please," he said as he started shedding the rest of his outer layers.

Rayna heard the snow crunch under another car pulling into her driveway and remembered her plans. "Damn."

"What?" Wolf paused mid-glove.

"That's either Sam or Barb. They're coming over to discuss our case."

"Oh, do you want me to go?"

"No!" Rayna almost shouted. "You just got here. If you want to stay and you don't mind shop talk, please stay."

Wolf finished taking off his glove. "I don't mind at all. In fact, you haven't told me much, so I'd like to hear all about it." Rayna rolled her eyes at the thought of him learning about her moment of fear in the barn, and he saw the action. "What?" He asked.

"Nothing. I mean you'll hear all about it," Rayna answered as she opened the door to greet Barb.

"Oh, good. I didn't have to wait for you to answer. It's colder out here than a witch's..." Barb paused when she noticed Wolf standing near the table. "Oh! Hey, Wolf! You're back!"

"Yes," he grinned. "Colder than what?" He asked.

"Never mind," Barb said and looked through the door toward the road. "It looks like Sam's here."

"Good," Rayna said and stretched her hand out to Wolf. "Let me take your coat." He handed it over and she turned to Barb who was shaking herself loose from her pink puffy jacket. "Yours, too."

"Where are you taking it?" Barb asked.

"I'm going to put them in the bathroom next to the little space heater. They'll be warm and toasty when it's time to leave."

"Ooh! Good thinking!" Barb said as she handed hers over.

Rayna left the room just as Sam entered. "Well, hello, Wolf. You're here!"

"Yes, I am," Wolf answered as he sat down at the kitchen table. "How are you?"

Sam grinned and nodded "Oh, I'm good. Just a little cold. How was Mississippi? And are you supposed to be back already? I thought Rayna said Tuesday."

"Mississippi hasn't changed much, but Mom is well, and yes, I told Rayna Tuesday. Then I decided to surprise her… and you, too, I guess." He laughed. "Don't mind me. I'm just here to catch up on all the excitement."

Sam was talking off his coat as he asked, "Why, what has she told you?"

"Not much yet, but I can tell there's something to tell. Otherwise, you both wouldn't be here on a work night."

"True, true." Sam replied.

Barb chimed in, "You won't believe it!"

Rayna rounded the corner as Wolf said, "Oh, really? Try me." She held her hand out toward Sam and he instinctively handed her the coat.

Rayna quickly left the room again, but called over her shoulder, "Really!"

Barb sat down at the square table across from Wolf and Sam sat between them to her left. "Where should we start?" Sam asked Barb.

Rayna answered from the hallway, "At the beginning!"

The team filled Wolf in on the investigation to that point. While they were talking, he kept his focus on Rayna who had sat down at the table between him and Barb, and she couldn't escape it. His gaze was intense, and she was sure that he, like her, wished they were alone. But she couldn't rush her friends out the door when there was an important matter to deal with, so she just smiled sheepishly and let them tell the story.

It didn't take long to get to the part about their experiences in the barn, and after describing Sam helping Barb exit, they handed the story off to Rayna, who was suddenly self-conscious. It was hard enough to admit being afraid and feeling vulnerable to her best friends but admitting it to Wolf felt like admitting defeat. She wanted him to think of her as brave and running from something she couldn't see didn't feel all that brave. She found herself speeding through the story to just get through it, and his deep blue eyes were wide when she finished.

"Are you alright?" He asked her.

"Yes, I'm fine. I'm still here, right?" She answered with an edged tone she didn't expect. "I mean, yes. It was just a weird thing."

"Indeed," Wolf said. "And you want to go back to get rid of this thing? Do you even know what it is?"

Sam answered for her, "That's what we're here to discuss. What could it be — the thing in the barn — and what's in the house? Also, what's with the weird marble with a mind of its own, and why would things start getting so intense now? I'm actually wondering if we somehow made it worse."

Those were all questions that had passed through Rayna's mind, too. In the past, clients had told them they were afraid just talking about paranormal events would somehow create more activity. While Rayna didn't normally believe that to be the case, this situation was already much different than any stereotypical haunting they had handled. "I had the same thought," she told them.

"Yeah," Barb almost whispered.

Wolf nodded in understanding. "So, what have you learned since then?" He asked the group.

Barb answered first, "Like Mandy told y'all in your first visit with her, her great-grandparents, Abraham and Lucy, owned the land. It had been part of the farm the family had initially worked as slaves. Somehow a while after the Civil War

83

ended, they saved enough money to purchase the property from their former...
um... owners." She looked at Sam for reassurance.

"Yeah, there's no way to sugar coat history when it comes to slavery," he said.
"And I'm glad you found their names."

"If they hadn't owned the property, I probably wouldn't have. So anyway, they
had it and gave it to Mandy's grandparents," Barb continued, "but it seems their
children weren't interested in living there. So, they sold it, but then Mandy came
back and bought it a few years ago."

Rayna added, "She was pretty proud to be able to do that. Also, didn't she say
the property was sold from under them? I wonder if she just didn't have the
family history right from memory, or if it was told to her that way. Anyway, she
thought her grandparents would have appreciated the property being back in
the family, but I'm starting to think maybe they don't like the idea so much."

Wolf asked, "Why would you think that?"

"Because I think the spirit in the house might be related to her, maybe even her
grandmother," Rayna answered.

"Or her great-grandmother?" Sam asked.

"Maybe," Rayna nodded.

Wolf asked, "Do you feel like it's a protective spirit?"

Rayna marveled at how he seemed to have his own level of intuition about
things like this, although he would never talk about his own sensitivity. "I do,"
she answered. "The more I think about it, the more I think whoever is in the
house is there to protect her from whatever is in the barn. She said the only
things that happen in the house is the marble appearing where it shouldn't be
and moving about on its own, which happened here, too, seeing that shadow –
but sometimes it's more like a point of light – and the rocks being thrown

outside. I looked it up, and I think that's called *lithobolia*, or at least it was in the late 1600s when it happened in New England during Puritan times. It was considered a form of witchcraft."

"What wasn't?" Barb asked sarcastically.

"I know, right?" Rayna replied. "There's a story about that happening to an innkeeper on an island in New Hampshire, and it supposedly happened for months. He accused some neighbor lady that he was in a property line dispute with of doing it. She accused him of doing it to make her look bad, or something like that. Anyway, that was the only real example of it happening I could find on record, or at least online."

"So, we're on a witch hunt now?" Wolf asked.

"We?" Sam asked with a sly grin. "Are you joining us on this one?"

Wolf sat back in his seat and nodded. "If something threatens my girl, I'm not letting her go back there without me."

Rayna looked at him and smiled. She hadn't heard him use that phrase before, and she liked it. "Thanks," was all she could say.

Sam nodded, "I can appreciate that. We're glad to have you." Then, he looked back to Rayna, "Was your priest able to give you any guidance?"

"Some. He asked around and learned that instead of a demon, it could be a sort of thought-form called a servitor – created by magick with a *k*."

Barb asked, "With a 'k'? Do you mean like witchcraft?"

Rayna nodded.

"So, we *are* on a witch hunt?" Sam repeated Wolf's question.

"Of sorts. Learning who created it and why, assuming that's what it is, will help us figure out how to deal with it," Rayna answered.

Wolf added, "And it might have been created long before your client was born."

"You think?" Sam asked.

"I know. Well, sort of. I've heard stories of created entities that took on a life of their own and continued to survive long past their creators."

Rayna's jaw dropped. "You have?"

"We don't call them servitors, but it's a similar idea. It's created to serve a purpose, usually something that would benefit the creator, but it's dark magic, and it just gets darker," Wolf explained.

"So, why do you think this one was created?" Sam asked.

"Either there's something in the barn – or was something in the barn – that it's protecting, or it was made for some sort of revenge," he answered.

Rayna said, "I think it's a prisoner of the barn."

Barb asked, "Why do you think that?"

"I found out what those weird markings on the door are," Rayna answered. "They seem to be a type of sigil used for protection. The design is called a hexafoil, and it's been used for centuries as a way for folks to shield themselves from dark magic. You can even find it in stained glass windows in some churches, which is why it looked vaguely familiar to me."

"If it's trapped in the barn, maybe we should just let it stay trapped in the barn," Sam said. "I'm not sure we're equipped to take this thing on."

"If it had been a demon, would you say the same thing?" Rayna asked.

"No, I would have let the priest handle it," Sam answered.

"My priest couldn't handle it. At least, not on his own. Priests have to be trained in the rite of exorcism. He's just a simple parish priest who finds all this fascinating."

Wolf asked, "Do you think he'd be interested in helping?"

"Only by preparing me for whatever course of action we decide to take. This really isn't his cup of tea."

Barb asked, "So? What do you think we should do?"

"We need to find out the servitor's purpose – assuming that's what it is – who created it, and when. That may help us figure out how to send it away," Rayna sounded confident, but in her heart she wasn't certain.

Sam asked tentatively, "What if it's not a servitor. What if it really is a demon?"

Rayna shrugged. Then we're going to need more than a little folk magic to send it off."

Wolf spoke up, "If it's a thought-form as strong as it sounds, a little folk magic won't be enough."

"I was afraid of that," Barb said.

Wolf asked Rayna, "What do you do when you clear homes of human spirits?"

"I smudge with a sweetgrass and sage stick, and then I bless the house with holy water."

"Does it work?" He asked, knowing the answer.

"Yes, as far as I know. The clients I've done it for reported that it did." She wasn't sure where he was going with this line of questions.

"That's more than a bit of folk magic. You're combining Native American cleansing with Catholic prayer. That's stronger than putting random objects in a bag and burying it under the doormat." Wolf told her.

"Wait," Rayna stopped him by holding her hand up. "What did you just say?"

Wolf cocked his head to one side. "Why? What?" He could tell he'd triggered an idea.

Rayna answered, "That's a gris-gris bag, right? Putting random items, usually in odd numbers, in a bag and using it for protection. Is that what you're talking about."

Wolf nodded. "Yes, I've heard it called something else, I think, but I can't remember what."

"And you bury it under the doormat?" She asked.

"That's the popular spot, but it could be anywhere, I guess. The door is the entryway to the home, so it makes the most sense to put it there."

Rayna slapped her hands on the table. "That's it! That's the marble, I bet. I mean I bet the marble was in a gris-gris bag. Mandy keeps finding it near the back door. When I had it here, it moved on its own to my back door. Or something moved it there, but you know what I mean."

Sam asked, "Do you think it had been buried near that back door to protect against what's in the barn?"

Rayna nodded enthusiastically, "I do. That door is the closest doorway to the barn. I wouldn't be afraid of the thing walking through the front door. It would travel the shortest distance it had to."

Barb asked, "How do we prove that's the case?"

Sam answered, "Dig under the doormat and see what else we find?"

"I'm not sure Mandy would be excited about us digging up the space around her back door. Plus, if it were buried decades ago in a fabric bag, that fabric might have disintegrated by now." Rayna told him.

"True," Sam said.

"Why don't we just ask her if she's found anything similar outside near the door?" Barb asked.

Rayna looked at Sam, "Could you call her? Oh, and ask if she thinks Lucy would be looking after her."

Sam glared at Rayna, "Why do I have to call her?"

"Because you got us started down this road," Rayna pointed at him, grinning. "That makes you the client liaison for this case. Also, can you ask if it's been quieter inside the house since we returned the marble?"

"Okay, okay." Sam got up and walked into the living room to make the call.

Rayna turned her attention back to Wolf. "How do you know so much about folk magic and servitors and all of this spooky stuff? And why didn't you tell me about this side of you?"

Wolf sat back in his chair with a sly smile, "I wanted you to be the expert in spooky stuff. Plus, you've never asked."

Rayna was dumbfounded, so Barb took the opportunity to ask him, "What else do you know about? I mean, as a ranger, do you get Bigfoot reports? What about alien big cats like black panthers? Werewolves?" She had a tinge of excitement in her voice.

Wolf laughed. "Yes, yes, and no."

Barb took the bait. "Have you *seen* Bigfoot?"

"Only when I look in the mirror," he laughed as he pointed to his boots by the door.

"Ugh," she sighed. "I thought I was going to get some dirt."

Rayna laughed. "Barb, he's seen aliens. Isn't that enough?" Barb nodded, and Rayna asked Wolf, "What else do you know about that I should know about?"

"I don't know," he answered. "I guess we'll just have to see as these things come up."

"Oh, great," Rayna said. "I'm hoping this particular thing is a one-and-done." There was a lull in the conversation that gave her time to process everything. Eventually, she asked Wolf, "Do you think smudging and blessing the barn would work if we can't learn anything more than what we already know?"

"It might, but let's hope we learn more. I'd rather go in with confidence than feel like we're literally taking shots in the dark," he answered.

Sam returned to the room and took his place at the table. "I hope you're all free on Saturday," he told them. Each one nodded slowly. "Good because that's when Mandy wants us to do something about her problem."

"Oh, no," Rayna said. "Has it gotten worse?"

Sam answered, "Well, she said that first night it was pretty quiet, so she thought having the marble back helped. But Sunday night, it was wide open. Rocks, shadows, even whispers in the house. She made her daughter come stay with her, and that poor woman just wants to go home and sleep in her own bed."

"Why doesn't Mandy go to her daughter's house and stay there?" Barb asked.

"I asked the same thing. Her daughter yelled from the background – I guess I was on speaker phone – that Mandy is too stubborn for her own good."

"I can relate," Rayna said.

"Yeah," Sam continued. "Anyway, she's had her fill and wants us there as fast as we can get there. I told her Saturday would be the soonest since we all have full-time jobs. She understood, but she told me not to chicken out."

"I guess we need to be prepared for anything on Saturday," Rayna said.

Barb wrinkled up her nose and sighed. "I'm not going back in that barn. I don't care what y'all think of me." Her voice shook when she said it.

Rayna reached over and patted her shoulder. "You don't have to. We'll work on the house first, and then you can sit in there with Mandy and Kendra. You'll be fine there." She looked at Wolf, "Can you help me in the barn?"

"Of course!" He answered without hesitation.

"Okay." Then she looked at Sam, "In that case, you can stay in the house, too."

"Oh, now wait a minute," he crossed his arms.

Rayna held her hand up with her index finger raised. "Wait, Sam, before you get your feathers ruffled, if anything happens in the house when we're in the barn, I need you in there."

"I thought you just said you'd do the house first."

"I will, but that doesn't mean it might not need more. It's hard to know with two distinct issues at once, how things will play out."

Sam relaxed a little. "Okay, I guess that makes sense."

Barb questioned Sam, "Did you ask her about Lucy?"

"Yes, and she thinks Lucy could be the presence in the house, but she doesn't understand why her great-grandmother would be acting that way."

91

Rayna closed her eyes for a moment and heard the answer as clearly as if someone in the room said it out loud. "Because we stirred up the thing in the barn, and it's doing its best to target the house."

"So, Lucy's mad at us?" Sam asked.

Wolf answered this time, "I bet she's not happy with us, but more than that, she's mad at the thing in the barn and she's not strong enough to do anything about it."

Rayna looked at him and tilted her head sideways. "I'm pretty sure you're right. Psychic?"

"No," he said, "I'm just thinking how a protective grandparent from over 100 years ago might think. I'd be a bit grumpy, too."

Sam said, "Yeah, that makes sense, I guess." He looked at Rayna and added, "Bring your garden shovel. She thinks if there was a gris-gris bag that it would have been under the old oak tree, which apparently fell during a storm and barely missed the house. She thinks her grandparents would have reburied the bag near the back door if that was where they thought it should have been to begin with."

"So, we have permission to make a mess of her back entry way?" Barb asked.

Sam answered, "She said whatever it takes to quiet her home. I don't mind doing the digging, but the only shovel I have is a snow shovel, so that won't work."

"Okay," Rayna said.

"Don't worry about it," Wolf told her. "I have one in my work truck. I'll bring it, and I'll drive so you can just focus on whatever you need to focus on when we head over."

Rayna understood what he meant. "Thank you," she told him.

Sam clapped his hands together and asked, "So what else do we need to know?"

Barb answered, "Who created the servitor, when, and why, and how does Rayna and Wolf... de-create it? That's not the word I'm looking for."

Rayna laughed. "Destroy it might be a better verb."

Barb nodded, "Yeah, destroy it. That sounds more like it."

Chapter 10

Because Wolf had surprised Rayna a day early, he had to take a rain check on her cooking dinner for him, so he returned on Tuesday evening. She made beef stew in the slow cooker, and they spent the evening talking about all that had happened during his visit with his mother. For the first time since he had left town, she didn't mind the early sunset so much. Having him there lifted her spirits. Snuggling helped.

The workweek continued, and Rayna spent her time between forecasting and writing weather articles, learning as much as she could about servitors, hexes, curses, and anything else that might be related to the case. On Thursday night, she visited the church again to make a general confession to Father Martin. He reminded her to pray for Mandy's ancestors, pray for spiritual strength, and ask Saint Michael for assistance.

"He's really that active in the world?" She asked the priest about the archangel.

"More than you can imagine."

"How will I know if he's there?"

"You'll feel his presence," Father Martin told her confidently.

She thought about it for a moment and asked, "Do you know what that feels like?"

He paused and then smiled. "In my experience, angels don't bring the warm, fuzzy feelings you'd expect. I usually feel a chill when they're around – almost like a cold breeze without the airflow."

Rayna remembered the initial cold tremor she experienced when she first entered the barn during the investigation. "Mom always said if I had an intense chill that shook me from one shoulder to the next that an angel had walked over my grave."

"So, you have felt an angel?"

"Maybe? I mean if that's the feeling, at least in the context of that barn, it makes sense. That was the feeling I had immediately upon entering but it was just for an instant."

"Your guardian angel was probably trying to warn you that being in there was dangerous."

"I wish he or she... whatever... would have just said it out loud. I hear better than I used to."

"Clairaudience?"

"Yes," Rayna nodded. "I used to get everything intuitively or through physical sensations, but lately I've been..." She stopped.

"You've been hearing voices?" He asked.

She looked down at her hands in her lap. "I mean, I'm not crazy, Father."

He chuckled. "Rayna, don't worry. I understand that it's a gift. You're using God's gift to you to help others, so in my book, that's far from crazy. It's a blessing. The more you work with it, the more you're blessed."

"I guess." She laughed quietly.

Father Martin took a small card of about two inches by three inches from his pocket and handed it to her. "If you haven't yet, recommit this to memory, and use it on Saturday."

Rayna took it and studied it. On the front was a photo of a stained-glass window showing an angel with a sword holding it against the neck of what Rayna was sure was meant to be a demon, struggling under the weight of his foot. "Saint Michael," she said as she flipped the card over to reveal the most popular prayer invoking his aid. "I've said this before, a long time ago."

"It's one of the most powerful prayers I know, besides the Lord's Prayer, of course."

She put the card in her purse. "I'll recommit to it."

"Good," he said. "Do you need anything else from me?"

"No, you've been a great help. Thank you."

He stood to leave and said one final blessing over her with his right hand hovering just above her forehead, "May the Lord bless you and keep you, and may Saint Michael protect you and your friends as you act as God's witnesses on earth." He made the sign of the cross over her, and she crossed herself at the same time.

"Amen," she said. "Have a good night, Father."

"You, too." He started walking away, and turned back around to tell her, "Sit here as long as you need to, but please lock the door and turn off the lights on your way out."

"Yes, sir."

Rayna sat in silence for a while, appreciating the calmness that had overtaken her. She looked at the altar and the tabernacle and thought about how much those symbols meant to millions of people around the world. If they only knew how much more there was to the spirit world than they allowed themselves to think about. Too many people go to church so they can win a place in heaven without thinking of what their place on earth should be, too.

She took the card out of her purse and read the prayer to herself a few times. Then she replaced it and picked up a Bible that was sitting on a stand nearby.

She closed her eyes and said a prayer before opening it, "Lord, show me what I need to know for my work on Saturday." With her eyes still closed, she opened the book and let the pages fall where they wanted to. Then she opened her eyes and smiled at what she saw. It wasn't the first time she had opened a Bible to a page in the Book of Tobit, Chapter 6.

> Now listen to me, brother; we will speak about this girl tonight, so that we may arrange her engagement to you. Then when we return from Rages, we will take her and bring her back with us to your house."
>
> 14 But Tobiah said to Raphael in reply, "Brother Azariah, I have heard that she has already been given in marriage to seven husbands, and that they have died in the bridal chamber. On the very night they approached her, they would die. I have also heard it said that it was a demon that killed them.
>
> 15 So now I too am afraid of this demon, because it is in love with her and does not harm her; but it kills any man who wishes to come close to her. I am my father's only child. If I should die, I would bring the life of my father and mother down to their grave in sorrow over me; they have no other son to bury them!"
>
> 16 Raphael said to him: "Do you not remember your father's commands? He ordered you to marry a woman from your own ancestral family. Now listen to me, brother; do not worry about that demon. Take Sarah. I know that tonight she will be given to you as your wife!
>
> 17 When you go into the bridal chamber, take some of the fish's liver and the heart, and place them on the embers intended for incense, and an odor will be given off.
>
> 18 As soon as the demon smells the odor, it will flee and never again show itself near her.

Rayna closed the Bible and smiled. "Yes, sir," she said with her eyes raised to heaven. "It may not be a fish's organs, but I've got some nice sweetgrass and sage."

That night, as Rayna prepared for bed, she asked her spiritual helpers – angels, spirit guides, and beings of the light – to show her anything she might need to know for Saturday. It was a request she occasionally made when she felt like there was more that she needed to know about a situation. Any information about the spirit in Mandy's home or the dark thing in the barn would be appreciated. Rayna knew that receiving messages while she slept was often easier than when she was awake because her science-mind tended to get in the way when she wasn't dreaming.

Her request was answered, and her dream started with the usual random mix of images and symbolism of what she called a brain-dump from recent days. There were weather maps and friendly faces, a coffee pot that wouldn't brew, and sitting at her kitchen table laughing with her family. Then things changed, and she found herself standing in Mandy's living room, watching as a petite female figure materialized in front of her. The woman was middle-aged and African. She spoke English well enough, but didn't say much more than, "The marble was mine. The children are mad."

"Who?" Rayna asked her.

"The children. They don't want us here," she said as she pointed toward the back of the house. Then, the marble dropped from her hand and rolled toward the back of the house where the woman pointed.

"Are you Lucy?" Rayna asked, but instead of an answer, the woman faded into the background, and Rayna woke up. She looked at the clock on her nightstand,

and it said 3:33. She sighed and thought about the dream for a moment. It had to be Lucy, but whose children was she talking about? Hers or someone else's?

Rayna whispered a quiet "thank you," to no one in particular and added, "I'll figure this out in the morning. I need sleep."

When she started dreaming again, she was standing in total darkness and aware that she was not alone. Somehow, she knew that she was in the barn, and fear was pulling at her from all sides. "No," she said as forcefully as she could make herself, but her voice came out quiet and weak. "I'm not afraid," she said, again it was almost a whisper despite her trying to yell into the darkness. Then, she felt hot breath in her face, and her heart started racing. She felt something in her right hand and realized it was a small cigarette lighter, so she flicked it on.

The small flame illuminated the darkness around her just enough to show a shadowy dog-like face with deep red eyes just inches from her nose. The lighter went out, so she tried to flick it again, but it wouldn't light. She fought panic as a low growl surrounded her all at once, and she forced herself to stand firm. "I don't fear you," she said, again just a whisper. "I have friends."

Above her, a pinpoint of golden light appeared and floated down between her and the dark entity she knew was still there. It started to grow from a tiny point to the size of a marble, and Rayna was so fixated on it that she forgot the terrifying presence on the other side of it. She watched it grow to the size of a grapefruit and then a beach ball, and as it grew the growl faded. The light was filled with a powerful energy that seemed to flitter and pulsate from within. As it continued to become larger, she realized it was lighting the area around her and the darkness had retreated from her. Calmness overtook her and she understood she was protected. And then, her alarm buzzed.

She woke immediately and was a little perturbed because she wanted more from that dream. The feeling of peace she had reminded her of the stories she'd read of near-death experiences. It was as if she was going into the light, but that thought wasn't as soothing as it probably should have been. Did that mean the thing in the barn had killed her in the dream? She wasn't prepared for that thought. In fact, that was the last thing she wanted to consider.

The problem with receiving information in dreams is there is nearly always some level of interpretation required, and both dreams left her with as many questions as answers.

Chapter 11

Rayna's Friday morning dragged on as she tried to focus on forecasting yet another Arctic blast. The early winter had been unusually brutal for eastern Tennessee and knowing that Saturday's forecast was for more freezing temperatures and another chance for snow soured her mood. She thought back to her conversation with her sister about the message in her Christmas card. If winter was normally a dark season, this one felt like the blackest of night. And the dream about being in the barn seemed to cast even more shadows on everything. Was it even possible to be killed by a servitor? How much harm could a non-physical being really do?

She'd read of possession cases in which the victim was physically tormented, but she'd convinced herself that what was in the barn wasn't a demon. It had to be a thought-form of some twisted sort, and from what she learned from the first dream, it was created in anger by "the children," but whose? What kind of children had that kind of power? It sounded like something out of a Steven King novel. Her logical mind tried to tell her it was just a dream, but her instinct told her that both dreams had the messages she'd asked for. She just wasn't sure she had the right interpretation, and that was starting to shake her confidence.

When she broke for lunch, Rayna texted Wolf, "Have you ever heard of a servitor killing a person?" She waited a while before putting her phone down, realizing that he was working and not likely to reply quickly.

So, she googled it, and she found a few stories about physical injuries caused by thought-forms, but they seemed to have an air of creepy pasta – the term used for copied and pasted scary stories that never seemed to be grounded in truth. Rayna knew there were creepy pasta stories like that all over the internet, especially on websites that grew in popularity for outrageous and horrific claims. It was hard to trust anything from an anonymous source.

She decided to take a different approach to the dream and googled "seeing a golden orb." The first page of the search engine showed a mix of UFO reports and links to grainy alleged ghost photographs. She scrolled quickly past those and clicked to page two. Those results were a little more promising, and one near the bottom of the page caught her eye, so she clicked on the link and began reading.

> Golden-white light often represents beings of higher vibrational energy such as ascended masters, angels, or the divine being. In fact, working with archangelic energies is often called working with white light. Those who channel this energy channel the power to heal the world around them.

That paragraph led Rayna down a rabbit hole as she followed link after link to information about working with angels and realized there was a whole subculture of what many would call the New Age movement that claimed to work with Saint Michael in particular. She set her science-mind aside and decided to read with an open mind some of the incredible claims of healing and sending trapped spirits to the light. An hour after she started, she returned to her work with an improved mindset about the coming events.

Thirty minutes later, she received Wolf's answer, "No. Don't worry, sweetheart. We've got this."

That evening, Rayna met Sam at the good diner for dinner because he told her he had something she needed to see. While they waited for their food, he was excited to show her some old newspaper articles he'd found from the late 19th century. "I was digging in the archives when I should have been working on this silly little fluff piece they assigned me for the new year," he explained. "And I found these. The datelines are all Vickerton, and taken as a whole, the three of them create a narrative about a witch who lived in the area that had hired herself out to help people take revenge on those who'd done them wrong."

He pushed three photocopies of old print articles across the table toward Rayna. "Seriously?" She asked as she brought them closer to look more carefully.

"They're pretty short. Go ahead and read them. I'll give you time." He took his phone out of his pocket and started playing a game.

Rayna read through the articles as quickly as she could. They described an older African American woman who'd been accused of witchcraft. While there wasn't a law against practicing any religion, there was a law in place prohibiting the use of supernatural means to cause injury to a person or property. Rayna found that fact surprising but was relieved that they at least weren't drowning innocent women to prove they were in league with the devil. This person, named Henrietta, had a reputation for being able to hex people and cause them to leave their homes in fear. While the details seemed obscured by the writer, the gist of the story was that she wasn't denying she had the power to do it, but she wasn't admitting to causing harm to anyone. Most of her alleged victims were black people who had purchased property from a particular family in Vickerton. The story didn't name the family but alluded to their prominence and how after the Civil War, they'd been forced to sell off much of their land to pay debts.

The waitress brought Sam and Rayna's food just as she finished reading the third story. "So," Rayna asked, "do you think this is our culprit?"

"I do," Sam said with a prideful smile.

"Who do you think the family is?" She had an idea but wanted to hear his answer.

"The family that's buried in the little cemetery behind Mandy's house. From what else I could gather, their father had made poor business decisions and had to sell off parcels to his former slaves for pennies on the dollar. The stories said he did it with the hope that they'd make something of the land where he couldn't, so he didn't seem to have an ill will about it, but his children were not happy. They didn't want him selling their inheritance and even worse, they didn't want him selling it to black people they used to own. They even tried suing the buyers, but the court actually sided with the new owners, which, in that day – well, the court siding with black people was pretty unheard of."

"Wow!" she said. "Your ancestors put up with a lot of crap."

"Yeah, but at least mine weren't cursed," Sam said.

"True."

"I think his kids went to that witch and paid for a hex to be put on Mandy's great-grandparents."

"That makes as much sense as anything else." Rayna thought for a moment as she took a bite of her BLT. "In fact, it makes a lot of sense after my dreams last night."

Sam looked intrigued. "Dreams? Do tell."

Rayna described both dreams to him and explained how she thought she had the second one figured out, but the first had not been very clear until that moment. "I think you're right about the kids. I think Lucy knew it was them, and she created the gris-gris bag to protect their home against the hex."

"Do you think she carved the hexafoils into the barn doors?"

"I don't know. Maybe Abraham did that, or maybe someone else did in an effort to help them. I'm guessing Henrietta wasn't the only folk-witch around back then. There's been stories of Appalachian witches around here since well before the Civil War. I think most of them used what they knew to help people. This one," she pointed at the papers in front of her, "just went down the wrong path."

"I'm guessing it was easy money with all the angry white folks around here back then."

"I'm sure you're right."

"She betrayed her own kind for cash," Sam shook his head in disgust.

"I bet she was paid well, too, because it seems she must have been the real deal. Whatever she created outlasted her – at least we know one did anyway."

"So, what's your plan tomorrow?"

Rayna thought for a moment, "It hasn't changed much. We see if we can find the gris-gris bag, or what's left of it," and try to put Lucy to rest. Although maybe if we take care of what's in the barn first, Lucy will leave on her own. I think she's only there because she thinks Mandy needs her protection."

Sam nodded. "That makes sense. Do you still want me and Barb to stay in the house with Mandy and Kendra?

"I think that would be best," Rayna told him.

"I do, too," Sam reassured her.

The pair finished dinner and parted ways for the evening. Rayna went home and pulled out her rosary for the first time in years. If a priest told her to pray the Marian prayer for any reason, she'd consider it, but for the work she had ahead of her, she wasn't going to take any chances. When she finished praying the Rosary, she paused and retrieved the Saint Michael prayer card from her purse and studied it. She wanted to make sure she had every word committed perfectly to memory because she felt they'd only have one chance to get it right.

Chapter 12

Saturday morning brought low gray clouds and more frigid temperatures. Rayna added as many layers of fabric between her skin and the outside world as she could. Whether the barn's unnatural heat would be present was yet to be seen, and the unusually cold temperatures everywhere else were becoming unbearable to her. Her philosophy was that she could always remove layers as needed, but it was better to be over-prepared. Still, she had to laugh when she looked in the mirror and felt she was shaped like a giant fleece snowperson.

Wolf arrived at 10:30 AM to drive her to Mandy's. He was using the work truck with snow tires and seat warmers, and Rayna could not have been more thankful. They were meeting Sam and Barb at Mandy's house, so they could talk privately on the way.

"Have you ever done anything like this?" Rayna asked Wolf.

"Not exactly."

Rayna thought about his answer for a moment and followed up with, "How do you mean 'not exactly'?"

I've used sage to smudge spaces, and I've prayed for evil to leave my family alone, but I've never walked into a barn on a bitterly cold December day and tried to destroy a 100-plus year old, angry thought-form created by an old witch's hex."

Rayna nodded, "That's fair." She stared out the window. "I guess there's a first time for everything."

Wolf laughed. "You could say that!"

"Will you be comfortable with me saying Catholic prayers while we do a Native ritual?" She looked at him to see his facial reaction to the question, and he didn't hesitate.

"I'll be okay with whatever you do and whatever you ask me to do. I'm here to help, and if our combination of spiritual practices has the potential to work, then that's what we need to do." He gave her a reassuring smile and reached over to hold her gloved hand. "I have no doubt we can do this. Just because it's never been done doesn't mean it can't be done."

"Right," Rayna nodded and took a slow, deep breath. "Everything this week has told me we can do this, but we have to ask for help from Saint Michael."

Wolf squeezed her hand. "If he's our guy… er… angel, then, Saint Michael, please help us."

"It might be a little more complex than that," Rayna told him, and then she laid out her plan for their work in the barn.

When they arrived at Mandy's house, Sam and Barb were already there, warming themselves inside. Kendra had made hot cocoa for everyone and was bringing it from the kitchen as Mandy opened the front door to greet them. Rayna noticed that she had decorated her home for Christmas, and between the lights on the small tree in the far corner of the room and the flames in the fireplace, the whole place had a cheery glow to it. In fact, Rayna felt more like she was arriving for a holiday party than for driving out an evil entity. Somehow, though, it felt right.

"Hi, Mandy, I love your decorations!" She said as she stepped inside.

Mandy nodded and said, "Thank you, and who is this nice-looking fella behind you?"

Rayna, turned with a grin and presented Wolf. "Mandy, this is Steven Wolf. He's here to help me take care of your little pest problem in the barn."

Mandy shook Wolf's gloved hand and stepped aside so he could enter the warmth of the room. "It's nice to meet you, ma'am," he told her.

"My little pest problem?" Mandy asked. "Is that what we're calling it today?"

"It seems appropriate," Rayna answered. She took off her gloves and hat as she looked around the room.

Kendra offered them mugs of cocoa and motioned for them to have a seat on the couch. "Rayna," she said quietly, "Thank you for that little pep talk you gave the Reverend last Sunday." She looked over at her mother who was making small talk with Wolf. "Whatever you said worked."

"It did?" Rayna asked incredulously. "I was pretty sure he hated me by the time I left."

"Maybe, but last night, he called Mom and told her she was welcome back to the church whenever she was ready."

"Is she going back?"

"Yes, and it put her in such a good mood that she was up most of the night decorating the house for Christmas."

Sam overheard their whispers and leaned over to say with a wink, "Let's count that as our first Christmas miracle."

"First?" Kendra asked.

"Yes, the second will be whatever Rayna does in the barn." Sam pointed at Rayna with a grin.

"Let's just take it one step at a time, Sam," Rayna told him. "Oh, and there's a shovel waiting outside for step one."

Mandy heard that part as she walked closer to the whispering trio. "What's step one?"

Sam answered her, "We're going to do a little digging around your back door to see if we can find the source for your mystery marble, if that's still okay with you."

"Oh, yes. Yes. This time of year, I don't use that door much anyway. It's always muddy back there." Mandy told them. "So, you think my great-grandmother – did you say – buried a hex bag back there?" She asked Sam.

"Yes, ma'am, that's our current hypothesis." He looked at Rayna to explain, "Before you got here, we were explaining that we think Miss Lucy is who's in the house and that she's just trying to look out for her great-granddaughter."

Mandy pointed at Rayna, "Do you really think that's who's in my house?"

"Yes, ma'am. In fact, I'm pretty sure of it. Do you happen to have any old photos of her? Do you know what she looked like?"

"Oh, I do, somewhere. I'd have to look in the old albums in the bedroom," Mandy said.

"Was she petite?" Rayna held her hand about 4 feet off the ground, "I mean really petite with darker skin?"

"How did you know that?" Kendra asked.

"Yes!" Mandy answered excitedly.

"She was in my dream the other night and let me know the marble was hers. After that, a lot of our ideas about what was happening here finally fit together," Rayna answered.

Sam added, "It's like putting puzzle pieces together between Rayna's intuition and abilities and Barb's and my research."

Mandy pointed at Wolf, "And what part does he play?" She asked.

He answered for himself, "I'm just here to help Rayna with pest control." He grinned at the metaphor.

"You're Native American, right?" Mandy asked.

"Mom!" Kendra exclaimed.

"Oh, don't worry about it," Mandy told her daughter. "It's not like it's a bad thing. I'm just curious if that helps with these things."

"I don't know if it helps any more than any other heritage," Wolf answered. "It just means I've heard our folklore and have an open mind about certain aspects of our world that not everyone is willing to admit exist."

Sam drank his last sip of hot chocolate and motioned to Wolf, "If you're ready, let's grab that shovel and see what we can turn up."

The two put their hats and gloves on and stepped out the front door. As soon as it closed, Mandy reached over and patted Rayna on the knee, "Girl, he's impressive!"

Rayna blushed and looked at Barb who had been sitting in a chair quietly watching. Barb laughed, "We might have told Mandy you were bringing your boyfriend today."

Rayna nodded. "No wonder you were so quiet over there. Just soaking it all in, huh?"

Barb smiled. "I'm just enjoying this wonderful cocoa."

"Now, Rayna," Mandy said, "While the men are digging, tell me about that dream. I'll go grab my album while you talk."

Rayna described the dream in as much detail as she could while Mandy briefly went to her bedroom and returned with an old blue album that had seen better days. She sat down next to Rayna and started flipping through the pages and stopped when she got to an old sepia-toned six-by-four photograph of a middle-aged couple standing in front of the same house.

Mandy pointed at the image. "This was Abraham and Lucy, my great-grandparents who purchased this land and built this house."

Barb leaned over Rayna to see the picture. "Oh, my! She was short," She observed.

"Yes, that's where I get my genes from, obviously," Mandy said. "Abraham looks tall by comparison, but he was really just average height."

Rayna was aware that Lucy was present and felt the need to compliment her. "Lucy's dress is very nice here. It looks pretty fashionable for the time."

"Yes," Mandy said, "I'm sure that was her Sunday best. It wasn't often you had your picture taken back then, so you had to look your best when the opportunity arose."

Barb asked Rayna, "Is that who you saw in your dream?"

Rayna nodded. "That's not what she was wearing, but I'm pretty sure it was her."

They were interrupted by triumphant shouts and knocking on the back door. Mandy sprang up from the couch and said, "I hope that's a good thing."

"Sounds like it is," Kendra said as she hastily walked through the kitchen to open the back door.

Outside Sam and Wolf were all smiles. Sam was holding a muddy scrap of sackcloth up for her to see while Wolf grinned and filled in the hole they'd created. "We found it!" Sam said and handed it to Kendra.

Kendra examined it and walked it over to the trash can to brush the mud off it. "You found something. What do you think this is?"

Sam answered from the open doorway, "We think it's what's left of the gris-gris bag that little marble might be from."

Kendra looked at him and said, "Oh, don't stand there with the door open. Come in!"

Sam looked back at Wolf for the okay to leave him to his work. "I'm almost done here. I'll put the shovel back in my truck and come in through the front door," Wolf told him, so Sam stepped inside and closed the door.

Rayna, Mandy, and Barb joined them in the kitchen and watched as Kendra took the less muddy piece of cloth to the sink to rinse it off.

"Careful, there, Hon," Mandy told her. "It might disintegrate."

"No, Momma, it's pretty solid," Kendra replied. When she was done, she had a brownish-tan scrap of cloth that had a deep crease showing where it had once been folded. She handed it to Mandy, who held it up toward the ceiling light to get a better look.

"I can see where the thread holes were. This was definitely a handmade bag at one point." She turned to show the holes to Rayna and asked, "So, we found it. Now what do we do with it?"

Rayna thought for a moment and answered, "Do you have a needle and thread?"

Mandy seemed to know what her thoughts were and walked past her on her way to her bedroom. "Yes, I do."

Wolf came in the front door as Mandy went for her sewing kit. He clapped his hands together and asked, "Rayna, that was it, right?"

She smiled at him from the kitchen doorway. "Yes, I think that's it, but it seems like there should have been more than just a marble in it."

Mandy returned with a thick needle and brown thread. "This should work. I'm not sure I can do the sewing though. My hands get too stiff. Miss Rayna, do you want to do it?"

Before Rayna could answer, Kendra said, "I can do it."

Rayna liked that idea. "That's perfect, Kendra. I think it's fitting for someone in the family to mend it."

Kendra asked, "So, you think maybe there was more in this little bag? It looks like it was pretty small."

Rayna felt a twinge of guilt for what she had said. "Maybe," she answered, "that's all they had. I think it's more about intention than the number of items in the bag."

Everyone made their way back to the living room, but Rayna and Wolf didn't sit down with the rest of them. She stood close to him and whispered, "Are you ready?" He nodded without a word, his eyes reassuring as he looked into hers.

Barb noticed their exchange and asked, "Is it time?"

"Time for what?" Mandy asked as she turned to look at Rayna and Wolf.

Rayna answered, "While you're in here, Wolf and I are going to take care of what's in the barn."

"You never actually told me what *is* in the barn," Mandy observed.

"We didn't want to worry you anymore than you were already worried," Sam explained.

"Yes," Rayna affirmed. "Sam's right. From what we've uncovered, we think it's something called a servitor, and those markings, or sigils, on the barn door were put there to keep it confined to the barn."

"For the most part," Sam added, "they seem to be working."

"Oh, my!" Mandy said. "What exactly is a servitor?"

Sam let Rayna answer that question. "It's a sort of entity called a thought-form that is created by someone powerful enough to give life to an intense emotion. We think this one was created to get revenge on Lucy and Abraham."

"Wait. What?" Kendra asked, surprised. "Who would have done that?"

Sam answered, "I found some very old newspaper clippings about an alleged witch who lived around here in the late 1800s who had been hired by a prominent family to scare people out of their homes, specifically former slaves who had recently become homeowners."

Rayna watched Mandy's face for her reaction and saw a flash of understanding. "Yes," Mandy said, "I suppose that wasn't a popular thing for them to do back then."

Rayna told her with as much empathy in her voice as she could, "I think the witch cursed your great-grandparents, and they did what they could to keep the servitor at bay with the gris-gris bag," she pointed to the cloth Kendra was working on, "and the sigils."

"I see," Mandy said.

Rayna asked her, "Do you think that might be why your grandparents sold the property? Maybe they were tired of worrying about the thing in the barn?"

"Wait a minute," Mandy said. "They sold the property? Do you mean Abraham and Lucy actually owned it? I understood differently."

Barb answered her, "I found tax records that showed they owned it. That's how we learned their names. Then, your grandparents sold it and moved to town."

"It's just a guess that they were trying to escape the hex," Rayna said. "At this point, I'm not sure we can ever know for certain."

"So," Kendra asked, "why would the thing start acting up so much now?"

"I think Mandy buying the property and starting to fix the place woke it up, so to speak. I'm guessing the curse was on the family, and you're family." Rayna told her, motioning to the two of them.

"Okay," Mandy said with a sad acceptance. She looked around the room and then up toward the ceiling. "Great-grandma, I'm sorry. I didn't mean to start anything." Rayna saw her eyes glisten with tears and walked over to put her arm around Mandy's shoulders.

"Don't be upset. You didn't know," Rayna said softly. "She's happy you're here. She just came back to protect you."

"How?"

"The marble," Wolf told her. "Somehow the marble got separated from the hex bag, and she knew it needed to be put back."

Rayna added, "That's why she's been moving it. She was trying to tell you it was important, and when it was at my house, she tried to tell me, too."

Mandy looked shocked. "What? How?"

"It somehow jumped out of the bowl I'd put it in by the front door and rolled all the way to my backdoor. I didn't understand until this week that the backdoor to your house was the hint as to where the marble belonged."

"So, that's why I kept finding it back there?"

"I think so," Rayna said.

"Momma," Kendra interrupted, holding up the freshly mended sack cloth bag, "where's the marble now?"

As if in answer to the question, they heard the familiar sound of the marble hitting the floor in the spare room. Everyone's eyes got wide, and Rayna bolted into the room to find it under the desk where she had first met the little thing just a couple weeks prior. She reached under the desk and picked it up. It was cold to the touch, as usual, and felt like it was buzzing with energy. "Thank you, Lucy," she whispered as she walked back to the living room.

Kendra handed Mandy the bag, and Rayna handed her the marble. With a little flare and a silent prayer, Mandy put the marble in the bag and pinched the top closed. She waited a moment as if expecting some movie-style magic to happen, but everything was still except the crackling fire. "Okay," she finally said, "Is that it?"

Rayna answered, "I'm hoping that's it for inside the house. Now Wolf and I have work to do." She walked back over to where Wolf was standing close to the front door and put her knit hat and thick gloves on. "While we're doing our thing out there, I have one request for you in here."

"What is it?" Kendra asked.

"Think happy thoughts, share happy stories, and focus on everything positive in the world. Don't let darkness enter." And with that, Rayna and Wolf headed back out into the cold.

Chapter 13

As Rayna and Wolf walked around the house and made their way to the barn, Rayna wove her arm into the crook of his elbow, and he looked down at her with a warm smile. "I really do think you're awesome," she told him.

"I feel the same about you," he said and gave her a kiss on the forehead.

The weight of their purpose was weighing heavily on Rayna as they paused before opening the doors to the barn. She watched as Wolf pulled a large bundle of wrapped sage, a lighter, and a turkey feather from inside his jacket. Then she pulled a large shell out of her coat pocket and handed it to him. "Thanks," he said.

"Before we go in, I think we should say a prayer." Wolf nodded and they both bowed their heads. "Heavenly Father and Creator," Rayna started," Please, protect us in your white light and positive energy. Insulate us from negativity and help us to be conduits of your light where it's needed."

Wolf raised his eyes to meet hers as they both said "Amen." Then he said, "I thought you were going to pray to Saint Michael, no?"

"I'm saving that for inside if we need him."

"If?"

Rayna shrugged. "Maybe the marble was stronger than we thought?"

That hope was dashed as they opened the doors to the barn and the growling started before they crossed the threshold. She looked at Wolf and shook her head. "Or not," she said.

They left the doors open for the smudging ritual. The idea was to let the sacred smoke make all that was evil leave through the doorway. "Where should we start?" Wolf asked.

"We need to work the perimeter first, right?" Rayna asked, trying to ignore the constant low growl that seemed to emanate from nowhere and everywhere at the same time. She noticed the same unusual warmth they'd experienced the week before. "Do you feel that?"

"The heat?" Wolf asked. "Yeah, it's like you said."

"Yeah," Rayna looked around. Even with the doors open, much of the barn still seemed dark as night.

They went to their right, still close to the entrance and Wolf, holding the shell and the smudge stick in one hand, lit the sage and waited for it to start smoldering. But the tiny flame barely got going before it went out. He lit it again, holding the flame to the sage a little longer. "Too cold?" Rayna asked.

"Not in here," he said. She watched as he tried again. This time, it stayed lit and after a moment the smoke began to flow up from it in thick gray tendrils. He put the lighter in his pocket and used the shell to catch any ashes that fell and the feather to start wafting the smoke toward the wall of the barn – up toward the ceiling and down toward the floor.

Rayna started repeating her favorite smudging mantra, "Only light and love are allowed in this space. All darkness and hate must leave." She said it a few times before the growling grew louder. Her first thought was to pause, but she knew that wasn't right, so she said it louder. "Only light and love are allowed in this space. All darkness and hate must leave." Again, the growling's volume increased. It seemed to fill the air and she could feel a rumble in her chest as if she were standing in front of giant speakers at a rock concert. Wolf felt it, too, and started repeating the mantra with her as they slowly made their way past the first corner and down the long side of the barn.

The farther they went into the building, the darker it became. Wolf couldn't see the smoke anymore, but he could smell it and trusted the sage was still smoldering. Rayna stayed close to him, touching the back of his jacket for

118

reassurance as they continued to repeat their intentions. Then, she smelled it – the rank odor of rot and sulfur. Her heart was in her throat and her voice faltered. She gave Wolf's jacket a little tug to get his attention, and he turned around to see her eyes wide with fear. "Do you smell that?" She asked.

He paused, sniffed, and then wrinkled his nose. "I do now, thanks." He held the sage up to his nose to mask the stench and realized the embers had died. He took the lighter out and lit it again, and again, it wouldn't stay lit.

Rayna was trying to stay focused on Wolf but could feel an intense pressure in the center of her back. It wanted her attention and wasn't going to take no for an answer. The image of those red eyes in her dream came back to her and she took a deep breath, immediately regretting it when the foul odor filled her nose. "Ugh," she said. Wolf continued to struggle to light the sage.

"Let me try," she said, and he handed her the lighter. She focused on it and tried to will more energy into it. Then she flicked it on under the sage. This time it lit, but quickly went out.

"This isn't working," Wolf said in frustration.

"No, and the thing is right here," Rayna said motioning toward her back. Wolf looked around her and squinted. "I don't see it."

"Trust me," she told him, "I feel it." He nodded. "Plan B?"

Rayna thought for a moment and took his hand. With all the courage she could muster, she turned and guided him toward the center of the barn. She felt the servitor step back and watch them pass, and in her mind's eye could see its dog-like face grinning as it thought it was winning. When they got to about the center of the barn, she told Wolf to face her and hold her hands so that they created a small circle between them. He obeyed and she said, "we're going to pray to Saint Michael now." He nodded, and she started the prayer. "Saint Michael, the Archangel," she paused. The words escaped her. She knew the prayer by heart and could say it in her sleep at this point, but she couldn't remember it at that moment. "Damn it!"

Wolf understood and gave her hands a light squeeze. "It's okay. Clear your mind and start over. You've got this."

Before Rayna could try again, the growl transformed into a low, mocking laugh. Wolf's face betrayed his shock, but he quickly shook it off and nodded at her to go ahead. She shook her head to loosen her neck and shoulders and started again. This time the words came more easily. "Saint Michael the Archangel, defend us in battle. Be our protection against the wickedness and snares of the devil; May God rebuke him, we humbly pray; And do thou, O Prince of the Heavenly Host, by the power of God, thrust into hell Satan and all evil spirits who wander through the world for the ruin of souls. Amen." As she said it, the laughter turned back to growling and was louder than ever. It filled her ears, and she couldn't hear Wolf telling her to try again.

"Why isn't it working?" She screamed in frustration.

He shook his head and looked around the room. "Something's missing!" He yelled over the noise.

"I said every word!" Rayna's heart was beginning to race, and she felt like she was losing her nerve.

Wolf let go of her hand and snapped his fingers, and then pointed to his eyes. "You have to see it!"

"What?" She asked.

"Visualize what you need to happen!" He waved his hand around his head and the motion jogged a memory.

For a moment, she could see the small pinprick of light from her dream and then instantly remembered a golden light meditation she had read the day before. "Oh! I've got it!" She grabbed Wolf's free hand to reconnect their circle.

The growling had turned to a roar and the pressure on her back was becoming so intense that she felt like a wall of hatred was slamming against her. She closed her eyes to refocus, and this time as she started the prayer, she imagined that pinpoint of light coming down from above them to the space between them. "Saint Michael the Archangel, defend us in battle." The roar intensified and was joined by a fierce wind. She felt like they were standing in the middle of a severe thunderstorm. "Be our protection against the wickedness and snares of the devil," she envisioned the light between them growing more quickly than it did in her dream as the wind tangled the curls of her hair not covered by her cap. Wolf's long, black hair was whipping around his face as he continued to focus intently on her. "May God rebuke him, we humbly pray." She felt the temperature noticeably drop in the space between them, or she thought she did. She felt a chill run from her chest through her body to her back and goosebumps formed on her skin under all those layers of clothes. "And do thou, O Prince of the Heavenly Host, by the power of God, thrust into hell Satan and all evil spirits who wander through the world for the ruin of souls." She saw as if it were really there, the ball of light between them turned into a burst of energy and broke out of their circle. The roar became a pained howl and the wind felt tornadic as she watched the white-gold orb spin around them in a circle with a tail like a comet. It whirred past their heads, and she realized it was moving in concentric circles gradually spreading away from them toward the outer edges of the barn. As it did, the air around them cooled and the barn became easier to see. Rayna looked up and saw what looked like a whirlpool of golden light swirling above them. "Do you see that?" She yelled over the cacophony.

Wolf was looking up, too. "I do!" His answer relieved Rayna because the whole thing felt too big for her imagination.

The howl became a wail peppered with shrieks as the comet of angelic light reached the edges of the barn. The doors slammed closed, startling Wolf and Rayna. They grabbed each other and held close as the wind tore at their coats and rattled the walls of the barn. Surprised, Rayna realized despite being cut off completely from their source of sunlight, the barn was fully illuminated. She and Wolf both looked around and then up as the wail became a whine and the whirlpool of light began to shrink.

"Dear God," she said as they watched it close in on itself, shrinking to a pinpoint of light and then blinking out. Simultaneously, the sound ceased, and the wind stilled. The doors of the barn swung open to reveal bright sunlight, and they stood in silence, just staring out into the world, still holding each other in a reassuring embrace.

"Amen," Wolf finally said.

"Amen," Rayna repeated, and she buried her head in the warmth of his jacket.

He squeezed her shoulders and asked, "Are you alright?"

She lifted her chin and nodded, "Yes. Are you?"

He stepped back and patted himself on the chest, back, and head. "All in one piece!"

They looked around the barn as Rayna did a sensation check. Everything seemed normal. The barn smelled like old hay, she could hear birds chirping outside, and the air was frigid again. Wolf seemed to be noticing the same details. They looked at each other for a moment, and then Rayna yelled enthusiastically, "We did it!"

"Yes!" Wolf agreed.

"Well, we had help," she said, pointing toward the ceiling.

"What *was* that?" Wolf asked incredulously.

"That was Saint Michael and his Merry Band of Warrior Angels," she told him with a sense of pride in their work.

"Merry band of...?" He stopped himself. "Well, okay then."

Rayna laughed and grabbed his arm. "Let's go inside and see how they fared!"

As they got to the doors of the barn, Rayna pointed at the carved hexafoils. They were glowing as if lit from inside. "Look at that!"

"Wow!" Wolf got closer and watched from inches away as the light faded to black and the symbols seemed to almost disappear into the old wood. "Amazing."

"Absolutely!"

They stepped out of the barn and closed the doors. Rayna noted how much brighter the interior looked and felt, even as they shut the sunlight out. Outside, the clouds had rolled away, and the early afternoon sun was almost blindingly bright, warming their faces and making Rayna wish she had one less layer of fleece on. She realized she was sweating from the unnatural heat in the barn, and maybe a little from nerves, too.

Before they walked into the front door, they paused and hugged one more time. "Thank you," Rayna told Wolf. "I couldn't have done this without you."

"I think you could have," he said, and she shook her head in disbelief. "But I'm glad I could be here for you." He gave her a little squeeze and a quick peck on the lips before she turned around to open the door.

Inside, Sam, Barb, Mandy, and Kendra were all laughing heartily. They turned when they heard the door open. Sam's smile faded as looked at his friends with concern. Everything about Wolf and Rayna seemed disheveled and even tired. He asked, "How'd it go?"

Rayna and Wolf exchanged glances as they took off their hats and gloves. Rayna answered, "I think it went well, but it was a little wild there for a minute."

Mandy asked, "Wild?"

"Yes, ma'am," Wolf said. "If you notice anything out of place out there, you can blame us. I don't think anything was broken."

"Could you not hear it from here?" Rayna asked, realizing how clueless the rest of them were.

"Hear what?" Barb asked with Kendra echoing her.

Rayna looked at Wolf and shrugged. "I guess not. Interesting," she thought out loud, and tried to decide how much detail they really needed. "Let's just say that the servitor didn't go without a fight, and for a moment, I wasn't sure who was going to win."

Mandy rose from her chair and walked over to the two of them, "So, it's gone?" She asked.

"Yes, ma'am." Wolf said. She opened her arms to hug him, and he bent down to let her. Then she turned to Rayna and embraced her, too.

"Thank you! Thank you so much!" She had tears in her eyes as she said it.

Kendra stood and walked over to hug them, too. She got to Rayna first and gave her a bear hug. "Thank you for helping my momma." When she stepped back from the embrace, she asked "What about Lucy?"

Rayna looked around and tried to tune into Lucy's energy, but there was nothing there. "I think she's moved on."

"Oh, hallelujah!" Mandy exclaimed. "Thank you, Lucy, and thank you, Lord," she said with her eyes raised toward heaven.

Kendra said a jubilant, "Amen!"

From the couch, Sam half-joked, "It's another Christmas miracle!"

"You can say that again," Barb agreed.

"Mandy," Rayna started, "You should have a peaceful home and a normal old barn now. I have no reason to believe anything else, but if you ever need us again, don't hesitate to call, okay?"

"I won't," Mandy replied. "Thank you again. I just can't thank you enough!"

The group said their goodbyes and left Mandy's house as the snow glittered in the sun. Rayna and Wolf sat in silence for the first half of the drive back to her house. She looked out the window at the countryside and enjoyed the peacefulness of it all. Wolf seemed to be doing the same. She finally broke the silence when she remembered her mother's invitation to Sunday dinner.

"My mother says you're invited to dinner tomorrow," she told him matter-of-factly. "Don't feel obligated, though. I mean, I'd like you to come if you want to, but…"

"I'd love to," he saved her from stammering on. "I do have to work the early shift, so it depends on what time."

"If I tell her that, she'll ask me what time you can make it. I honestly think you're the reason she's inviting anyone to dinner." Rayna laughed. "When you couldn't make it last week, she found an excuse to postpone it to this week."

"In that case," Wolf smiled, "tell her six o'clock is perfect." He reached over and took Rayna's hand, pulled it gently to his lips, and kissed the back of it. "I wouldn't miss it."

Nicolle Morock lives in the Triangle area of North Carolina and is an SEO content specialist by day and an author, podcaster, Reiki Master, and Certified Emotion Code Practitioner on evenings and weekends. She has a B.S. in meteorology and a B.A. in communication. Her hobbies include paranormal investigation and research, reading, traveling, and enjoying the flowers in her garden. Her roommate is Penny, a black cat who keeps odd hours and makes sure Nicolle takes time to play.

With over a decade of experience investigating the paranormal and a lifetime's worth of personal stories, she is uniquely qualified to write fiction and non-fiction about that subject.

Visit NicolleMorock.com to sign up for Nicolle's newsletter and check out her other creative projects. Newsletter subscribers receive a free short story!

www.ingramcontent.com/pod-product-compliance
Lightning Source LLC
Chambersburg PA
CBHW030132260626
47156CB00008B/2916